S.T.O.R.M
ECHO'S CALL

S.T.O.R.M
ECHO'S CALL

Maria Alice Gray

M.A.G

2020

Copyright © 2019, 2020 by Maria Alice Gray

All rights reserved. This book or any portion thereof may not be reproduced or used in any manner whatsoever without the express written permission of the publisher except for the use of brief quotations in a book review or scholarly journal.

First Printing: 2019

Revised Printing: 2020

ISBN : 9780244054229

CONTENTS

Acknowledgement..7

Introduction..9

1. Eye Of The Storm......................................17

2. Tipping Point...45

3. A Few Hours Earlier.................................60

4. Turning Point..81

5. Echo's Call..92

6. Heroes...106

7. Moving On...123

8. Delta Echo..139

Galactic Background..................................152

S.T.O.R.M Command..................................159

Operative Profile..165

ACKNOWLEDGEMENT

I tip my hat to Seán for giving me the nudge I needed to get S.T.O.R.M out of my head.

We might not have met in person, but the impact you made was just enough for me to challenge my preconceptions.

Thank you.

INTRODUCTION

S.T.O.R.M.

The quasi rescue-military organisation that is the backbone of the Delphinus Galaxy.

Since it first commenced operations on 19th Aratha 1946, S.T.O.R.M has played a vital role across the 12 realms of the cosmos. Whilst the organisation has evolved throughout its long and eventful history, its primary objectives have remained unchanged:

1# Provide rescue assistance wherever and whenever it is required

2# Provide combat backup to military forces when it is requested

3# Give hope to those who need it

4# Stay strong in the face of despair and adversity even if the odds are against you

5# To never ignore a call for help

S.T.O.R.M's mission: **To be there**

Nowhere is this more clearly stated than the organisation's signature motto, *"we've got your back."*

At S.T.O.R.M's core are its field operatives; highly trained versatile rescuers who join S.T.O.R.M from various walks of life. From generational operatives to academics, ex-military, medical staff, teachers and many more, each sentient joins S.T.O.R.M to serve and protect the Delphinus Galaxy.

S.T.O.R.M is divided into 7 branches.

S.T.O.R.M Command is the central branch, managing the administration responsibilities of the organisation and galactic communications. It is also the branch of the all rounder field operatives, known better by their nickname 'mercies'.

Located in the Hurricane System is the S.T.O.R.M Academy. The S.T.O.R.M Academy focuses on the training of field operatives and call responders, preparing them for their dutiful lives. Known as 'demmies', trainee S.T.O.R.M field operatives typically spend between 2 – 4 years at the academy before graduating.

S.T.O.R.M Medical is the second largest of the organisation's branches. Sharing Base Lempra with S.T.O.R.M Command, S.T.O.R.M

Medical focuses on personnel and operative care, field operations and galactic outreach. The field operatives for the branch are known as 'paras'; an abbreviation of the Alingu word paramedic.

S.T.O.R.M Engineering oversees any and all engineering developments and operations that concern S.T.O.R.M, playing a vital role in keeping S.T.O.R.M active across the cosmos. Known best by their nickname 'gennies', S.T.O.R.M Engineering field operatives tend to join S.T.O.R.M from engineering or military backgrounds, with an increasing number joining straight from academic studies.

The smallest of the S.T.O.R.M branches, S.T.O.R.M Military's role within the organisation is geared more towards the care of its field operatives, as opposed to providing a service to the Delphinus Galaxy.

Sharing the planet Lantos with S.T.O.R.M Engineering, 88% of S.T.O.R.M Military's field operatives, known as 'millies', join S.T.O.R.M from military service, both demobbed and active.

Regarded as the greatest branch of S.T.O.R.M, the 'guardies' of S.T.O.R.M Guard are the most beloved of all. Set up by the original 12 field operatives on 2nd Yyenn 1950, the branch was named after S.T.O.R.M's 13th field operative; a Tyerria Retriever canine named Guard.

S.T.O.R.M Guard features a strong diversity of operatives from across various branches of the animal kingdoms. These include canines, felines, avians and aquaforms such as dolphins and sharks. Guardies always partner operatives from other branches, living life in the field alongside their fellow operatives, who in turn take care of them.

Created at a much later date than the other 6 branches, S.T.O.R.M Strikeforce, or simply Strikeforce, was created on the back of the 2275 L'Xarian System massacres.

Over the years, Strikeforce's role has expanded to include upholding The Guardian Angel Accords; the galactic law that protects S.T.O.R.M's field operatives. They also oversee policing of the Rochdale and Chase systems.

Due to its smaller size, all personnel and field operatives within Strikeforce hold a call sign, regardless of their status and active roles. Their nickname 'strikers' is a play on the first part of their branch name.

Each S.T.O.R.M branch has its own field operative call sign set and secondary colour.

S.T.O.R.M Command utilises the original set and secondary colour of eagle yellow whilst the other branches, bar Strikeforce, use call sign sets put together by the original field operatives.

S.T.O.R.M is led by its Operations Director who decides the relevant courses of action for the organisation. At present Sara Narusha; S.T.O.R.M Tango Delta, holds the position. Taking over the role in 2390, Sara also speaks on behalf of S.T.O.R.M in any and all galactic matters that concern her organisation. She also has regular contact with The Unity; the governing body of the Delphinus Galaxy.

Sara is amongst the best known operatives currently serving, but she isn't alone. A number of field operatives are also galactically well known.

Stand out names include S.T.O.R.M India Juliet; Harmony Alonso, a former Galactic Tournament athlete whose extreme sports vlogs for the S.T.O.R.M Connect project entertain billions of fans across the cosmos. Participating in sports ranging from bike tracking, deep sea dives to space jumps, India Juliet pushes the boundaries.

S.T.O.R.M's deputy director, S.T.O.R.M Alpha Lima; Wynona Sorbonne, rose to popularity when her base Eagle Station

1. EYE OF THE STORM

CAUTION.
CAUTION.
CAUTION.

"I see it, *Sweet Remedy*," Jack assures her trusty navy blue starship, effortlessly piloting the battered spacecraft to starboard.

Her bright yellow cheatlines shine almost neon in the planet's stormy pink atmosphere as her blonde-haired, blue-eyed veteran pilot clocks yet another encroaching hazard.

Fighting invisible savage winds, *Sweet Remedy* manages to skirt around yet another of the dull grey spheres that blanket the area. In the churning cerise maelstrom their menacing shapes loom like silent voids. Jack knows all too well the price of contact with them. Dense ionised gas could be *Sweet Remedy's* death call.

The veteran operative's hawk-like eyes continue to scour the turbulent unyielding skies, looking for even the slightest glimmer of bioluminescent hide. Her ears strain to hear the vocal calls of her rescuees, their quiet calls lost somewhere deep within the crackling static and thunderous roars of the deadly maze.

From behind Jack's right ear a stray golden strand falls free of her ponytail.

She ignores it.

The bulk of her ponytail is secured away beneath her grease adorned flipped back electric blue S.T.O.R.M cap.

Jack's attire is basic today even by her lax standards. In the early hours of the morning she threw on whatever was closest to her when she awoke. It amounted to a surprisingly clean navy blue t-shirt with yellow sleeves, her famous call sign printed on the left sleeve, electric blue and eagle yellow utility trousers and duty belt clean on from yesterday, plus her preferred EVC boots, the colours matching the trousers.

Jack transferred her metal insignia pin onto the t-shirt, placing it on the left hand side. Since the inception of S.T.O.R.M it has been an unspoken rule to always have your metal pin on your uniform. To not do so is unthinkable for a S.T.O.R.M field operative.

"Where are you my wayward friends?" Jack murmurs to the angry skies.

Static, thunder and gusting roars greet her.

Navy blue fingerless glove clad hands grip tighten on familiar manual controls, Jack's fingers perfectly slotting into the wear grooves on the starship's silver joysticks.

For years the engineers of Eagle Station have been offering to replace them, but for Jack the worn grooves offer an assurance of control and a chance of winning.

As Jack Fact 9# clearly states: Jack always does the impossible.

Even Jack can't deny that.

The irritating static increases tenfold over the commlink as *Sweet Remedy* dives beneath another sphere of death.

Heavy turbulence continues to jostle her as she continues with her mission, the violent atmosphere of the hostile planet no place for any starship within S.T.O.R.M's extensive fleet, let alone an RPM Class.

But this is no ordinary outing.

WARNING.
WARNING.
CORE TEMPERATURE CRITICAL.

"I know, Rems," the mercie replies calmly.

Even at critical temperature Jack knows *Sweet Remedy* will be fine. What the starship hasn't twigged are the non-computer measures Jack put in place around her computer core.

Sharply she banks her girl to port, only just avoiding another of the ionised spheres. A crosswind pushes and pulls the starship in a momentary tug of war for control, releasing her abruptly back into the battle for survival.

White lightning clashes to and fro.

High winds continue to rush at the starship.

Her flaps work overtime to compensate.

Ahead lightning forks out like a web across the horizon, almost blinding as a roar of thunder hits her a few seconds later.

Jack might not be outwardly religious, but she sends a quick prayer to the val'kii goddess of life, praying that *Sweet Remedy* avoids another lightning strike. She isn't sure if she can restart her girl again if *Sweet Remedy* takes another direct hit. The last lightning strike almost overloaded her navigational array.

Not that that has been much help.

Jack has been flying blind with only her starship's proximity sensors, whatever scanners decide to work sporadically, and her own steel-blue eyes to keep her girl in the air.

Sweet Remedy is taking a right battering on this mission. So much for a simple code blue mission on Stellaris Day!

Things just had to take a turn for the worst.

A flash of white lightning brightens *Sweet Remedy's* darkened command deck for a spilt second.

Jack prefers it dark when she's piloting like this; the darker it is the better she reacts. The only light around the lowered pilot station coming from the visual displays and consoles in various bright colours.

The rest of *Sweet Remedy's* spacious navy blue and eagle yellow command deck is lit by the low glows of monitors from her duo of starboard stations and her single port side engineering station, accompanied by the sharp white lines of her emergency lights in the deck's floor and ceiling and the soft ambient glow of her main monitor bathing the deck.

Running the full length of the starboard side, right up to the closed off laboratory set at the back of the deck, Jack set the monitor to run on its own batteries, displaying a screensaver of the colourful dolphin-shaped cosmos that is the Delphinus Galaxy. It is usually a comforting sight to behold, but not right now as another sphere appears from the pink murk.

Jack avoids it with ease, swinging *Sweet Remedy* around to the sound of thunder and crack of lightning as it whites out the deck once more.

HULL FRACTURE DETECTED.
TIER 3 SECTION 2.

"That's a bit close to the hangar door."

Using her peripheral vision Jack checks the readout data on the console to her right, her primary vision focused on keeping her starship flying whilst finding their missing rescuees. The cockpit's viewscreen panels give Jack a clear ranging view of the danger zone outside, whilst the head up display offers her an array of mostly useless data in colourful readouts.

She counts her starship's lucky stars.

The hull fracture is indicated to be 25cm from the top edge of the main hangar door, 12cm in length.

Worrying?

Yes but nothing Jack can't fix with a bit of metal sealant later.

Whenever later is.

Sweet Remedy can handle this; she's a warrior in the face of nature's brutality.

A starship built to take a battering.

And this mission is adding to the starship's incredible tale. Her heroic operator has a part to play in that.

S.T.O.R.M Delta Echo, aka Jack Winters.

A veteran S.T.O.R.M field operative with 20 years to her call sign, the 5'4ft, square-jawed female human who is the favoured galactic hero of the present day, beloved by quadrillions across the entirety of the Delphinus Galaxy; this despite her typically operating inside the Lempra Realm.

But a hero is a hero at the end of the day.

A jolt from beneath is unexpected.

WARNING.
WARNING.
WARNING.

Jack remains calm and unperturbed by the conditions. She and *Sweet Remedy* have flown in many a storm of different kinds over the years. Jack has complete faith in her starship and the many hours of piloting they have clocked together.

Her eyes glance upper right to the neon green compass working overtime.

They are heading north again.

The altitude is correct also for once as Jack spares a brief glance down to her left at their neon blue readings. At least she's aware of her distance from the ground and space.

That's something.

A bolt of bright lightning crackles into life!

Sweet Remedy's main engines cut off.

"No you don't, Rems. C'mon reboot, it's just lightning. You can handle a surge," Jack calmly commands.

The starship responds immediately.

Her back up power generator fires up.

Her engine sequence cycles.

The head up display confirms victory.

The twin hums of her main engines cuts back in, the low groans reverberate through the deck as a blue confirmation lights up the head up display.

Jack brings *Sweet Remedy's* nose back up with a firm pull back of the twin silver joystick controls. The starship climbs deftly to a higher altitude, banking hastily to port once again to avoid a smaller sphere. She banks sharply to starboard to avoid another.

Jack certainly isn't planning to graze a sphere again; the first and only time she did she almost spiralled into a crash landing.

They don't need a lesson recap.

Nobody in S.T.OR.M's history has ever flown a starship into the atmosphere of a kilerra class planet before now.

For good reason too.

It was impossible until Jack, Kel and Turiso figured it out for their duo of starships.

Just 2 hours earlier Kel managed to briefly pilot his larger Discovery Class starship through Torero's savage atmosphere. *Graceful Angel's* flight might have only lasted 14 minutes 23 seconds with no happy rescue ending, but they still pulled off the impossible and escaped back to space relatively unscathed.

Jack and *Sweet Remedy* have the RPM Class honours, and they are being made to suffer for it.

A quick time check to the lower right screen reveals the chrono in neon yellow.

32 minutes 33 seconds.

MICRORACTURE DETECTED.
TIER 2 SECTION 17.

"Nah, that's just an empty bedroom, *Sweet Remedy*. Nothing in there but a bedspread and a book Sara gave me to 'better widen my understanding of holidays'," Jack dismisses with a smirk.

Whilst the younger veteran appreciated the kind gesture by her long suffering Operations Director, the notion of being away from duty for longer than absolutely necessary doesn't appeal to Jack in the slightest. S.T.O.R.M Delta Echo is a mercie on a mission, an operative on call, not a sunbather hogging a sunbed at a paradise resort.

"No thanks."

CAUTION.
CAUTION.
CAUTION.
WARNING.
WARNING.

"*Sweet Remedy*, I know this is torture for you but we need to find those leviwhales or else they're going to die, and no thanks to that. I'm not ending the year on a death note," Jack tries to reason with her starship.

2395 has been a relatively good year, bar that sandbar shark incident on Newfoundearth during the summer which did not happen.

At least according to Jack it didn't.

The official report says otherwise.

Of course she saw that pesky shark buried in the sand as she waded across the shallow river; it just moved suddenly meaning she accidentally stood on it and incurred a painful bite.

A gust forces *Sweet Remedy* off course!

Jack compensates immediately, turning her girl back into it.

The veteran mercie has pushed her girl hard on a number of occasions, but this mission is something beyond. In theory it should be beyond her operational capacity, not that that has ever stopped S.T.O.R.M Delta Echo and her incredible RPM Class starship.

In the early days of its testing, Jack had taken a keen interest in the new starship class. In the year it launched into active service, the RPM Class won spacecraft design of the year; just like its predecessor, the ageing Rapid Class.

The classes share a lot in common.

Same 3 tiered structure.

Same base layout.

Same rear end.

The same adoration by field operatives.

BANG!

"Hang on!" Jack shouts.

She is quick to jerk on the controls.

She forces *Sweet Remedy* out of her near lightning strike induced dodge dive, the winged starship banks hard to port, avoiding a sphere that gets in her way.

"That was nothing, don't worry about it," Jack dismisses casually to her starship.

"Who am I kidding? Everything in this atmosphere is too close for comfort," she admits to herself.

Her eyes check the structural scans to the left. Various red spots glow on the neon blue outline schematic of the famous starship.

The command deck has picked up a few microfractures, including a particularly large 30cm fracture above the lab. Jack has already sealed it off should the hull decide to rupture.

She also saw sense to seal off *Sweet Remedy's* centrally placed spiral staircase and starboard side elevator. It's not like she's going to run downstairs for a sandwich during this.

Her accommodations deck has faired a little better than the command deck; nothing major beyond microfractures and a scorch mark on the starboard side from a lightning strike. Though the additional shielding around the deck might be to thank for the lesser damage.

Jack winces at the third deck's scans.

Sweet Remedy's third deck has taken more damage than Jack would ideally like. Numerous microfractures and small fractures mar the starship's underside.

Whilst *Sweet Remedy's* hull is heavily shielded, the damage on her third deck is way too close to her vital systems and organs for Jack's liking. A direct lightning hit to that deck will end this mission quickly.

So far they've been lucky, but they have got to find those leviwhales as the starship continues on her rough rock and roll course.

Jack has never been a 'count the odds' type. She thinks of strategies then implements them, and right now she has gentle leviathans to save from a planet whose atmosphere has led them astray from their feeding migration routes. The leviwhales were on course to the galaxy's central twin suns before Torero placed them in serious jeopardy.

CAUTION.
CAUTION.
OVERSPEED.
OVERSPEED.

"Again with the overspeed warning," Jack remarks, "pick a different melody will you, Rems?"

Her hands turn the stricken starship to starboard to get out of the tailwind, dodging another sphere simultaneously.

Perhaps another operative may have looked at the odds and considered the leviwhales a lost cause. That wouldn't be held against said operative given what Jack, Kel and

Turiso have done is a fluke of experimental improvised mechanics.

Her blue eyes go to the neon yellow chrono once again; 35 minutes, 49 seconds.

Jack veers sharply to starboard.

CAUTION.
CAUTION.
CAUTION.
PROXIMITY DETECTION.

"We're going to clear it," Jack promises.

Sure enough they do.

Sweet Remedy manages to cruise over the top of the sphere with ease.

All around lightning continues to strike.

Thunder roars!

Winds buckle and crash.

And caught up in the middle is a starship that doesn't belong.

"C'mon leviwhales, where are you?" Jack murmurs, her eyes taking everything in.

Every churn of pink.

Every glimmer of potential information from her starship's barely functioning systems and readouts.

Every white bolt of lightning.

Every whisper of wind.

Every creak of metal.

Jack's metallic sky blue EVC helmet knocks into her left ankle. Even without the full Environmental Variable Conditions suit, the helmet will provide her with enough breathable air for at least 4 hours if it comes to that.

IF being the key word; Jack doesn't even know what the planet's surface looks like, let alone if it would be safe to land on, or even if *Sweet Remedy* could land and take off again after a crash.

Theory went out the airlock ages ago.

Sweat clings to Jack's brow in the humid air, her hands dry from her gloves, every sense on heightened alert.

Adrenaline floods her system.

Part of her is in awe of the vibrant light show outside. If it weren't for the danger and the mission, Jack would be intrigued by this strange world.

CAUTION.
CAUTION.
CAUTION.
WIND SHEAR.
WIND SHEAR.
WIND SHEAR.

"Shut up, Rems!"

A neon red and yellow warning flashes up, warning Jack of *Sweet Remedy's* dropping airspeed.

With the left foot control Jack boots it!

"Really, Rems? I would never have noticed because your audio alarms are too quiet," Jack sarcastically acknowledges.

As much as Jack loves her starship and wouldn't ordinarily backchat her, Jack knows *Sweet Remedy* well enough to not need the alarms.

Somewhere in the back of her mind Jack acknowledges that that comment will offend the RPM Class designer. Whilst Lynn Meicnic is a personal friend of the veteran, at least some of the time anyway, any insult to the RPM Class incurs her utmost wrath. Jack's persistent tinkering with *Sweet Remedy* incurs Lynn's wrath 100% of the time.

"We have test starships and procedures for this type of stuff, Delta Echo! You can't keep using your own starship!" Jack can hear her yelling from across the light-years.

Jack laughs out loud at the thought.

"Well I don't have a second starship to practise on!" Jack retorts back, smirking as she dodges a sphere directly ahead.

Sweet Remedy responds a little sluggishly.

A quick jerk to starboard then port seems to correct whatever the fault is.

"Problem 532," Jack notes, "Lynn's going to love this when we get back, Rems."

She often enjoys their verbal matches over what new upgrades Jack has concocted up and tested immediately on *Sweet Remedy.* For her it's just a show of how much they both care about the class.

Jack and Turiso had wondered what Lynn would think of their improvised lark for this mission. What they have done is certainly going to give her food for thought, perhaps a new mark of the RPM Class built for this conditions?

It wouldn't surprise Jack in the slightest.

Lynn had already proven her design prowess with 4x4 vehicles when she turned her green eyes to the growing medium-sized starship shaped hole in S.T.O.R.M's changing fleet. The ageing Rapid Class, S.T.O.R.M's last medium-sized all rounder starship class had long finished production. What started out as a new spec to give the Rapid Class a final outing became the RPM Class, the class proving itself beautifully when pirates decided to ambush the first prototype during its maiden space flight.

In the tempered turbulent atmosphere of Torero, Jack is finding the revolutionary twin joystick manual piloting system to be *Sweet Remedy's* saving grace.

Her hands tighten on the controls.

"C'mon, Rems, just a little weather issue," she murmurs to her girl.

Jack's glad she is alone this time.

Normally Harmony would be with her, with Rikos on occasion. Risking her starship in this hazardous rescue is acceptable in Jack's eyes. Risking another field operative for no good reason would have been a potential suicide mission. She'd tried to talk Kel and Turiso out of it, but as usual Kel saw through her, putting her back in her place via a rank call out.

S.T.O.R.M Sierra Tango is a captain.

S.T.O.R.M Delta Echo is a commander.

A streak of lightning flashes too close to *Sweet Remedy* for comfort as Jack skirts past another sphere, the sound of static dissipating unexpectedly for a brief second before returning with a vengeance.

"Might as well be looking for a needle in a hurricane," Jack states aloud as she eyes up a large sphere ahead.

She opts to dive below it.

A gust tries to side swipe the RPM Class into oblivion!

Jack compensates.

She steers into it.

Sweet Remedy makes her dive safely.

"Textbook," Jack calls out.

Her eyes look up to see the grey sphere pass, angry dark winds sweep its surface.

"I'm glad Harmony's not here."

KABOOM!

Sweet Remedy's head up display flickers in response to the too close for comfort lightning strike just to starboard.

Jack veers her to port.

"Definitely glad Harmony's not here," Jack affirms, "she'd be enjoying this too much."

Jack laughs.

Ordinarily the younger operative would be along for the ride but Jack forced her to take the festive period off. This was before Jack learned of the leviwhales mission; not that S.T.O.R.M India Juliet is missing out.

No sooner had they clashed over Jack's holiday double standards, Harmony received an invite to go snowboarding on the eternal snow planet of Hau over the festive period.

There was no way the tanned dark-haired mercie could or would miss up that type of an opportunity. The chance to visit a restricted world that only a small number were permitted to visit each year?

Sports junkie paradise!

The best part being it only cost Jack a bottle of Viper Strike she forgot she had onboard *Sweet Remedy*. The highly alcoholic beverage was a fair bribe in the eyes of the planet's caretakers, plus a photo with the famous S.T.O.R.M Delta Echo thrown in too.

WARNING.
EMERGENCY POWER LEVELS AT 94%.

"Buggar, we need to find them, Rems. Let's speed things up a rate otherwise we'll be here all day," Jack urges.

CAUTION.
CAUTION.
CAUTION.
WIND SHEAR.
WIND SHEAR.

"Problem 457 of 903, don't worry we've got this, Rems," she promises.

40 minutes.

Upper midpoint of Jack's provisional flight estimates. She isn't a fan of pushing *Sweet Remedy* like this but there is no way she is giving up just yet. Leviwhales are on the critically endangered list, therefore her beloved RPM Class can take the punishment for a little longer.

Jack knows she can.

"Those leviwhales have got to around here somewhere. We just need to get a fix on their location, a whistle, an echo, anything," Jack mutters aloud as she looks around.

Over the open commlink the near constant static continues to rein supreme like a mocking laughter of audio abuse, the noise sharp on Jack's hearing.

Sweet Remedy jolts up of her own accord!

Jack briefly wrestles with her controls, bringing the bucking RPM Class back under her control.

Fingers grip the controls tighter.

"Now now, let me do the piloting, Rems," Jack commands, "I'm know what I'm doing."

"I think."

S.T.O.R.M starships take a pounding.

That is the harsh reality of being rescue specification spacecraft. RPM Class starships in particular go through hell and back multiple times over the course of their lives.

Sweet Remedy is no different.

Whilst she has benefited from her operator being a technical genius of her class, *Sweet Remedy* has had more than her fair share of rough missions over her 14 years of service.

S.T.O.R.M RPM Class starships look alike as a rule, with their pearlescent navy blue paint and bright cheatlines, their insignias painted in black and white, positioned just behind their name on their starboard sides. The later specs of the class having slightly longer wings and different external guide light colours, but visibly they look the same.

Except no starship is ever truly identical, especially RPM Class starships. Each craft develops their own persona, added to by hull scars, operator touches, paint work and their own individual insignias, each as unique as their names.

This is where *Sweet Remedy* stands out.

The 14 year old starship is instantly recognisable with her bold eagle yellow lines, navy blue paint a distinct shade lighter than the standard RPM Class paint, and her veteran vibe apparent. Her insignia of a duo of leaping dolphins instantly recognisable.

A few scars mark her outer hull; reminders of her past missions. Scuffs around her hangar bay door, the faint marks of a plasma explosion on top of her command deck, tell tale usage marks around her starboard and port airlocks.

Most notable of them all is the scorch mark of a severe lightning strike to her starboard wing from a mission 7 years ago, the silver scar a striking contrast to her gleaming blue paint.

Jack has never had any of them resprayed. It remains an unspoken rule amongst starship operators; the story scars remain no matter what. Torero is bound to add to *Sweet Remedy's* as another lightning bolt lights up the thrashing pink skies. Jack will probably find it during *Sweet Remedy's* next dry dock session.

She gets shoved starboard by a ferocious sudden gust of wind!

THROTTLE UP.
THROTTLE UP.
THROTTLE UP.

Jack pulls back on the controls sharply!

She grits her teeth.

"C'mon girl!"

Sweet Remedy immediately responds, only just avoiding jagged black mountains that appear menacingly from the pink murk.

THROTTLE UP.
THROTTLE UP.
THROTTLE UP.

"C'mon, Rems," Jack urges as she climbs higher in a desperate bid to avoid even higher mountains, dodging to starboard to avoid another of the grey spheres.

As Sweet Remedy continues to climb, Jack breathes a sigh of relief.

"At least we know we're in a mountain range now," she observes as the mountains disappear into gloom once more.

A flash of lightning almost blinds her!

Blinking it off, Jack checks her instruments.

"That was nothing, Rems," Jack calmly announces as the blaring scarlet red Throttle Up illumination vanishes.

At least Jack hasn't hit anything major.

"Yet," she tells herself.

The unpredictable chaos of the atmosphere is proving to be both a test of her skills and her starship's integrity as more lightning flashes out across the horizon.

Sweet Remedy continues her mission.

But Jack's eyes catch a worrying sight flash up in red to her right.

WARNING.
WARNING.
EMERGENCY POWER LEVELS AT 92%.

"You're safe until 76%," Jack reveals to her starship, though in the back of her mind she knows the number is more like 81%.

She's pushing the limits.

Sooner or later she'll have to turn back.

Sweet Remedy can only take so much punishment, regardless of the lives at risk.

If only Jack had access to full power.

Sweet Remedy has to run on emergency power for this. It was the only way she could be protected with the shielding in place around her central computer core. Between Jack and Turiso, plus Jack's rather extensive engineering notes on the RPM Class, it was the only means they could think of whilst running on the absolute bare minimum of power.

"Where are you leviwhales?" Jack sings out, "S.T.O.R.M Delta Echo wants to guide you to safety."

The open commlink still refuses to offer up any audible clues to their presence. Just angry static of an inhospitable atmosphere greets her.

BANG!

The controls shudder in Jack's hands.

"Buggar!" Jack curses, concerned blue eyes going to the various readouts, her ears noting the increasing static over the commlink.

CAUTION.
CAUTION.
CAUTION.

Above right Jack clocks a new flashing red readout in a white rectangular box. A look to the neon yellow outline schematic confirms it: a major life support conduit has ruptured on the third deck.

"Buggar again!" she curses as a loud growl of rumbling thunder finally answers her leviwhale question, high force winds continuing to jostle *Sweet Remedy* like a toy boat in a lively child's bathwater.

WARNING.
WARNING.
EMERGENCY POWER LEVELS AT 90%.

"This is the first and only time I intentionally fly you into a kilerra class planet's atmosphere, *Sweet Remedy*," Jack promises.

She wrestles back command of her starship from the planet, banking her starboard once more, then to port then starboard again, annoyed eyes diverting their attention to the controls.

Something catches her attention ahead.

Steel-blue eyes go wide.

She jerks hard on the controls!

PULL UP.
PULL UP.

PULL UP.

"Yeah, I had noticed that!" Jack replies as a vortex of swirling cerise clouds forms directly below the fighting starship.

CAUTION.
CAUTION.
CAUTION.
WIND SHEAR.
WIND SHEAR.
CAUTION.
CAUTION.
CAUTION.

"Shut up already! I got this!" Jack snaps.

Banking hard to port whilst planting her left boot to the floor, Jack sends up a quiet prayer to any celestial deity presently listening, noting the tailwind *Sweet Remedy* has picked up and decided to tell her about in neon turquoise on the head up display.

CAUTION.
CAUTION.
CAUTION.

"This is beyond incredibility!"

The illuminated red warning *Sweet Remedy* opts to give her is overkill. All too clearly Jack can see the second growing tornado to starboard, just beyond it the ominous smoke black jagged shapes of yet more sky reaching mountains, grey spheres peppering the endless skies.

"How tall are these mountains anyway?" Jack asks aloud in surprise as she checks

Sweet Remedy's readouts, clocking the altitude jumping between levels.

"Well that's useful," Jack mutters.

A loud howl reverberates through *Sweet Remedy's* stormstricken hull as the starship rates the approaching storm on The Ekaitza Scale for measuring storm severity, offering a sound neon yellow estimate to scale.

Jack can see all too clearly that there is no way on Tyerria that tornado is only a level 3.

"That's powering up to level 5."

"Buggar, Rems!" she curses aloud.

The towering spiralling menace of pink clouds evolves faster right before Jack's eyes, growing larger and faster and stronger.

"Away from an angry tornado into another angry tornado; we're not having much luck."

Sharply she banks *Sweet Remedy* away from the storm, left boot still glued to the floor.

CAUTION.
CAUTION.
CAUTION.
PROXIMITY ALERT.
PROXIMITY ALERT.
IMPACT IMMINENT.

Jack agrees with her starship's warning.

She steers away to port, almost turning completely back on herself to dodge another grey sphere.

Another appears to starboard.

The tornado appears ahead.

Jack steers starboard.

She banks higher.

BANG!

In the blink of an eye all consoles go dead.

The head up display stripped of its power.

Engines power down.

Lighting fails.

Angry pink skies mottled with grey spheres replace the tornado as the stricken starship pitches downwards spiralling sharply into a chaotic clockwise dive. Jack reaches under the central piloting console with her left hand, fingers immediately landing on a much unloved red switch, flicking it twice.

The dead clicks are too loud in the air.

She tries again.

"No no no, come on, Rems, reboot. I know it's been a long time since we tried this method, Rems, but c'mon, reboot for me," Jack urges, attempting to do a manual fly-by-link reboot.

It has been years since they've done this.

The last time Jack remembers doing this was after *Sweet Remedy* got hit by an accidental ultrasonic pulse some 9 years prior.

Jack ensured they survived that.

They'll survive this.

She flicks the red switch again.

Nothing.

Jack flicks the switch a fourth time.

"C'mon, reboot, Rems," Jack pleads.

Still nothing.

Jack flicks it again and again as her starship starts banking sharp to port, completely outside of her operator's control and command. Dark looming mountains appear from the murk, dwarfing the starship, bathing her in shadow as she drops into a death dive.

KABOOM!

A flash of light greets her in finale.

"Another lightning strike, just as well the starship's dead," Jack notes absentmindedly as she continues her challenging task of saving *Sweet Remedy*.

"C'mon, Rems. We've got this; just another day on duty remember? We always do the impossible," Jack urges as a freak gust steers *Sweet Remedy* out of her death dive towards potential oblivion, levelling her off in open pink air.

Jack prays for another miracle.

She knows they've not completely used up their annual allocation just yet. What was it her beloved rewind Eric, aka S.T.O.R.M Echo Delta, joked to her?

"Sweet Remedy? Sweet Miracle more like."

Jack laughs at the memory.

Trust her beloved rewind to come out with something as daft as that.

But he wasn't wrong.

"C'mon, you're not being funny now, *Sweet Remedy*. I need you to wake up or we're both incurring hell for this," Jack urges once more, her concerned eyes now acknowledging the threat heading their way.

Or rather the threat they're rushing to meet.

Jack keeps trying as a particularly large grey sphere looms on their flight path.

On.

Off.

On.

Off.

On.

Off.

She resorts to Plan B.

THUMP!

BANG!

Jack has a microsecond to react!

A microsecond just in time as *Sweet Remedy* is yanked up by a sudden gust from below, slamming her back into higher air.

The grey sphere disappears to starboard.

Relief is only temporary.

BANG!

Under her harness Jack feels her organs slam forward. Her heart pounding in her ears over the roar of the planet outside her starship's hull.

The starship's upwards inertia slams into reverse with a vengeance, the powerless starship barrel rolling through the air as once again *Sweet Remedy* begins a death spiral, this time to port as deathly black mountains close in all around. Jack clocks another tornado somewhere close by as it whizzes past her vision.

Sweet Remedy is a hopeless passenger as the edges of the storm lick her hull, dragging her across to join the swirling mass of the tempestuous menace.

"The switch isn't going to work."

"Rems, we need another miracle."

2. TIPPING POINT

In her mind Jack runs over her options.

She has to get her starship operational again. She knows she can do an emergency power relay via the engineering station behind her, running it through the tertiary life support system batteries to the pilot station. It would mean abort mission but her life is worth more than this proverbial needle hunt.

Jack knows the score; a S.T.O.R.M field operative is worth a billion lives.

She has to escape Torero's atmosphere.

Return alive or else.

She knows Kel would literally find a way to kill her and reduce *Sweet Remedy* to scrap if they didn't come back from this mission.

Before the display went dead Jack clocked they'd been flying around for the past 45 minutes. In all that time Jack hasn't hear or seen a single hint as to where the leviwhales are. Better than that she's been attempting to find them in a starship not designed to handle the atmospheric conditions of a kilerra class planet.

"At least this gives everybody food for thought when we get back home," Jack reasons in mild humour, escaping her harness with a smack to the central buckle.

She pushes up from her seat.
BANG!
KABOOM!
Jack is thrown back into her seat!

Her head smacks loudly against its padded yellow headrest. Blinking rapidly to clear her head, Jack eyes her reward for attempting to get up, and it isn't a comforting sight...

"Oh hells no," she swears.

Blue eyes briefly glare at the disaster ahead. The surprise wind gust and lightning strike combo has knocked the starship out of the reach of the tornado, but it has placed her in a whole new world of trouble.

A colossal menacing grey sphere looms before them, growing larger and larger. *Sweet Remedy's* nose drops into a steep death dive, the turbulent air jostling her around like a rattle in the grips of a young infant.

Jack grips onto her seat.
Fingers dig in.
The sphere disappears only to be replaced with a trio of new death balls to port.

Sweet Remedy's nose picks up.
She levels only slightly.
Jack's view turns fully pink once again.

"This is not happening," Jack declares as she tries the red switch of miracles once more, her left hand clawing further into her seat in an attempt to stay in it.

Sweet Remedy pitches to port.
She pitches to starboard.

Her dive steepens.

She swerves side to side.

The trio of death balls disappear.

In their place a larger brother appears.

"This is really not happening," Jack denies.

Somewhere in the background her EVC helmet rolls off loudly, banging around as it hits a console or something.

Jack isn't paying attention to it.

What she is paying attention to now is the hazard growing larger in front of her eyes.

Her right hand desperately operates the little red switch, flicking it rapidly as a grey sphere looms directly in the starship's path, vicious winds dictating her motion in the skies of hell as she continues her rough descent.

Jack's temper finally starts to burn.

Quickly it builds into a bright rage.

"Dammit, *Sweet Remedy*! Can't you see what we're flying on a collision course towards you bloody idiot? Now is not the bloody time for you to take a frigging nap you sodding piece of scrap!" she snaps.

An angry thumping kick resonates.

"Kel better not check the black boxes after this mission; he'll have a heart attack from me saying that!"

The colossal ball of dense grey gas is amongst the biggest of the spheres Jack has seen in this hellstorm of an atmosphere.

The winds finally relent.

Sweet Remedy shakily levels off.

Delta Echo doesn't think next, she acts.

The turbulence threatens her with injury as she staggers over to the engineering station on the port side, almost falling back into the lowered pilot station.

The shaking does not to deter her as she cracks on with her task, kneeling down to yank off a yellow square cover on a lower console, exposing the silver and red coloured manual life support control junction beneath it.

Out of the corner of her right eye Jack acknowledges another of the grey spheres bearing down on the wounded starship, closing in like a scavenging predator.

BANG!

Black spots litter Jack's vision.

Pain flares at the front of her brain as it vaguely clocks she has been thrown forward towards the engineering station, her forehead impacting on the narrow padded edge. Padded yes, but still hard enough to induce a painful headache.

She tries to think it off.

Jack's vision blurs as she continues to scramble about. Shaking her head clear, she clocks the blue of the console as she tries to focus, the junction box little more than a warped red and silver painting.

She blinks her eyes rapidly.

"I don't need a concussion right now."

A final shake of her head clears her vision enough to work.

Jack works quick, transferring power from life support. She doesn't urgently need it given *Sweet Remedy* is liable to crash long before she runs out of air.

As if to prove a point the stricken starship pitches starboard sharply, sending her operator flying over the engineering station. Jack's scrambled mind clears just in time for her to see the outside view turn completely stormy pink, as if somebody has doodled on a chalkboard but then wiped clean all the marks.

Lightning flashes somewhere to port.

By some miracle a violent gust has forced *Sweet Remedy* off of her collision course with the giant grey sphere of destruction. But the danger is far from over as Jack picks herself up from her sprawled landing.

Sweet Remedy drops suddenly.

Only a single-handed death grip on the engineering station prevents Jack from having a flying session to the piloting station. Her head pounding from the motion.

"Oh give us a break," Jack mutters.

BANG!

The RPM Class flips, nose jabbing to the upper skies as she goes about her aerobatics. Jack's stomach churns as she tries to keeps her balance through the out of control manoeuvre.

The pilot station reboots!

Neon coloured information springs into life on the head up display, the sound of mechanic life hums through the command deck as lighting on the consoles and monitors flicker back into existence once again.

Jack throws herself at her pilot seat, strapping herself back in sharpish to retake control.

She pulls back on the joysticks.

Immediately *Sweet Remedy* responds.

"Thank the stars! We're joining them, *Sweet Remedy*!" Jack informs her starship, pointing her towards them and flooring the foot accelerator to maximum.

Sweet Remedy responds with a surge of power, mustering all she can with her engine exhausts 70% clogged.

Jack taps in a command to her right.

A corresponding amber illumination on the head up display confirms the attempted exhaust purge.

50%.

"It'll do," Jack assures the battered starship as she plots the escape route, steering *Sweet Remedy* to port around another sphere.

She has no shame.

This mission was always a long shot.

Jack knows she's done all she can to find the leviwhales, but she can't risk her starship in this planet's atmosphere anymore. She hates failing; no field operative wants to fail.

But Jack faces facts; *Sweet Remedy* has been looking for the leviwhales for 51 minutes 14 seconds. Once again she has gone above and beyond her operational specs, rewriting the

RPM Class operations manual whilst looking for a very small needle in a planet sized haystack.

The leviwhales are probably holding up better than she is given their thick hides protect them from almost all atmospheres.

Jack could take that as a small win if she were to focus on it, but she has been in the field long enough to know never to let your mind wander.

Mind on the moment: time and a place.

How many times has she said it over the past 20 years?

She lost count years ago.

The famous S.T.O.R.M mantra plays in the back of her mind like a well rehearsed song, the organisation's tune of ingrained talks, lectures and mentions.

The galaxy has S.T.O.R.M's motto.

The field operatives have their mantra.

Jack frowns.

Something doesn't feel right.

A high-pitched scream adds to the melody.

She spots the engine temperature gauges climbing on the head up display.

Sweet Remedy's cooling systems aren't doing their roles efficiently. Even with primary power offline they should still be running on their independent power supplies.

Her blood runs cold.

Sweet Remedy is heading towards a fatal cooling system overload!

"Buggar!"

Jack wipes her forehead on her right arm, the internal temperature of the command deck has climbed too, now a toasty 39° Theatus. The high internal temperature Jack can handle; she loves the heat, but the engine temperatures?

Her beloved starship being destroyed?

No chance!

The colourful gauges start to hit the top end of their optimal temperature ranges.

WARNING.

ENGINE SAFETY GUARD SHUTDOWN.

"No! No! No! Buggar! Don't do this!" Jack curses as *Sweet Remedy* shuts down of her own accord, her nose dropping immediately, twin engines whining as they run through their shutdown procedure.

"Buggar to hell and back!"

Jack taps furiously into the command pad on her right, trying to cancel out the sudden appearance of the defunct system.

"No, c'mon, don't do this, *Sweet Remedy*! Do not fall back on your test programming now! Not after all these years! There's no reason to reset to default!" she pleads.

Desperately she tries to fire her engines back up, trying to work the flaps, trying to dodge spheres and fierce winds.

"Grrr! Dammit! Safety mode! As if I didn't have enough to deal with already, this blighter of a system reactivates! Seriously?! Would it kill me to have something go right on this mission?"

Jack knows the drill.

All S.T.O.R.M starships run in safety mode for their first flight. If the flight is successful, the starship is signed over to its operator and the mode is deactivated.

And it stays deactivated.

"The weather has to be responsible for this, there's no way the system would have tripped," Jack mutters to herself.

She'll figure out the whys and hows later.

Right now she just needs her girl back online. Hopefully she can trip the system back otherwise *Sweet Remedy* will face a 20 minute reboot, with Jack having to be sat at the engineering station to do it.

Time is not a luxury they have.

Jack tries the remote switch once more, flicking it on and off as she manages to somehow get her starship almost level, the harsh weather and starship troubles making the task a true test of her piloting abilities.

Nothing.

She skirts a sphere to starboard.

Another to port.

Lightning flashes ahead.

Sweet Remedy won't glide forever.

Anything can bring *Sweet Remedy* down as her nose angles down slightly, skirting around a sphere by sheer luck alone. Even if nothing hits her on her rough descent, the RPM Class will glide to the ground and kiss it like a drunken field operative.

Despite the situation Jack keeps her cool.

Whilst this type of scenario has never happened before to her girl, Jack and *Sweet Remedy* have faced plenty of tough missions. If Jack had the chance to think, her mind would drift over their top 20 toughest missions.

Torero is going to make a rather big dent to the top 10 once they are out of here.

A memory does springs to Jack's mind.

Number 14 on the Top 20 list...

Or rather the solution to Number 14!

She acts on it, reaching for the small blue lever located next to the unloved reboot switch.

The little reliable lever labelled 'Emergency Automatic Flaps Release'.

She tugs on it hard.

The resounding *thump thump* sound indicates her success as the emergency hydraulics kick into gear. Jack allows herself a small smile as the telltale green light on her head up display indicates her success.

The flaps spring into life once more.

Jack smiles.

Small pressure sensors within the wings detecting what needs to be done, operating under their own automation. *Sweet Remedy's* flightpath stabilises as she continues her descent, her motion becoming less jerky in the air as she snakes her way into the lower atmosphere, the spiralling motion dissipates.

It's a start.

"Thank you code blue Mt Polaris mission," she praises aloud gratefully.

Many tests have proven a number of RPM Class operators react better than the automated flaps system, Jack included in that statistic, yet needs must sometimes.

WARNING.
WARNING.
EMERGENCY POWER LEVELS AT 87%.

Hands now free, Jack gets back to it.

Fortunately for *Sweet Remedy*, Jack Fact 7# exists: Jack likes to be prepared.

Switching to the backup systems she installed extra, Jack's efforts are rewarded with a green illumination to the right on the head up display.

Hopefully this will work.

If she can trip the command system the starship's engines will reboot.

At least, that's what Jack hopes.

These are extraordinary circumstances.

"Okay, now let's see if this works."

Jack taps the confirmation start up button to her left, but she gets no response from her starship's computers...an ear-piercing disaster inducing whistle screams from the console!

The stricken RPM Class plunges towards the ground in a steep dive, sucked down by a mix of gusting winds.

Jack wrestles commands.

Her starship once again spirals utterly out of her control, the flaps working overtime to stabilise her flightpath, a tornado spinning by as *Sweet Remedy* spirals around and around.

"Come back to me, Rems, please come back, c'mon," Jack encourages, retracting the automatic flaps release lever and returning both her hands to the main controls.

She wills her starship to listen.

Wills her girl to response.

Somehow she manages the impossible, bringing *Sweet Remedy* roughly level once more, but at a cost. Jack can feel the air speed drop away as she skirts around a smallish grey sphere, avoiding it by mere metres.

"C'mon fire up, Rems! You have got to do this!" Jack aggressively commands.

She tries the relaunch sequence on the forward piloting console, keying in a command to divert additional power to the cooling system from life support. Spotting the power transfer is complete she tries to restart her engines again...only to get scrambled feedback on the command.

"Great! I've fried the console cables!"

Jack goes again for the remote switch.

Nothing happens.

"Buggar!" she curses, "*Sweet Remedy*, if you don't cooperate with me, we're both going to die on this stupid planet and you don't want that!"

Jack's right hand goes again to the command pad, trying to fire up the stricken starship's engines once again.

Nothing.

No response from the engines.

No sign at all that the back up systems have seized control. *Sweet Remedy* is lost in an atmospheric ocean of crashing winds and engulfing clouds, the static of radio and roar of gusts echoing around her. At least with the engines offline the cooling system has been given a chance to cool off.

But it's the only blessing.

Jack relaxes in her seat.

She considers the inevitable as a strong wind tries to shove *Sweet Remedy* towards another sphere.

There's no denying: she is going to crash.

Or is she?

"This calls for an action of rather extreme violence," Jack declares in defiance.

With her right foot Jack boots the console!

The head up display flashes into life.

The engines restart with a hum and roar.

Power levels rise.

The starship's nose lifts.

Power surges through the deck.

The cooling system kicks into overdrive.

SAFETY MODE DEACTIVATED.
ALL SYSTEMS GO.

"Yes! Result!"

Jack retracts the flaps lever, counting her blessings the RPM Class has hydraulic back up systems. With a swift motion *Sweet Remedy* pulls up!

Jack breathes a needed sigh of relief.

"Welcome back, Rems," she greets.

She smiles as she checks the readouts, the starship continuing to steadily climb, allowing Jack a brief reprieve.

Sweet Remedy is still airborne.

Jack is okay, bar a few bruises and a future ticking off by a certain S.T.O.R.M Sierra Tango. The mild fuzziness in her head she can live with, along with the ringing in her ears. The leviwhales are still out there, hidden by cloud and static, but Jack dares not risk herself nor her starship anymore.

Her eyes clock the still counting chrono.

57 minutes and 59 seconds.

WARNING.

EMERGENCY POWER LEVELS AT 85%.

Jack laughs in response.

It couldn't have remained a simple code blue research-pursuit call could it? Things just had to take a turn for the worst and leap up the codes to a code white search-and-rescue.

Checking the readouts on the head up display, Jack notices the increased damage to her girl's hull, clocking a number of other microfractures that the starship hasn't informed Jack of. It doesn't surprise Jack in the slightest given how much the planet has been messing with *Sweet Remedy's* systems, along with her own head as Jack's vision blurs slightly.

She shakes it off again.

Steering around yet another ominous grey sphere, the battered starship continues her ascent to the stars above her.

"Almost home, Rems," Jack assures her.

The compass indicates them to be flying north-west once again. This entire time Jack has been flying on an estimated course, trying to guess the most logical path the leviwhales might have undertaken.

It was a long shot at the very least.

Like all field operatives Jack hates to fail, but she knows the first rule of rescuing better than most; you never save everybody.

All that matters now is getting her starship back alongside her mission sister and avoid getting her ear chewed off by her best friend. At least they did try something rather than just give up as soon as the leviwhales entered the planet's atmosphere.

If anything this mission is a technical win.

A stroke of engineering genius bound to leave a lasting impact on future design and safety of both the RPM and Discovery Class.

For the best Jack thinks as a menacing gust tries to blow *Sweet Remedy* off course. She compensates her battered girl's motion, stabilising her as she climbs higher yet, lightning forks close to starboard once again reminding Jack that the danger isn't over yet, not by a very long mile.

Yet despite it, Jack finds her mind fleetingly thinking back to the start of this disaster, how it turned from Kel, Turiso and herself simply minding their own business, to springing into full on action...

3. A FEW HOURS EARLIER

"Gosh! This is super boring!" the younger operative complains loudly, running a hand through his cropped black hair.

A loud tutting echoes across the deck.

"Those are not the words of a mercie, S.T.O.R.M Bravo Victor," Kel cautions him, the veteran operative's blue eyes remaining fixed on his console screen.

Turiso groans in response.

His exclamation doesn't come as any surprise to Kel. He just knew his rookie packmate was going to come out with something along the lines of 'I'm bored' sooner or later, but to give Turiso his dues, it has been 5 hours.

On the raised piloting station of *Graceful Angel's* silver and navy blue command deck, the young clyemnarian's ash-grey eyes scour the vast expanse of space ahead of them. His iridescent blue skin shines under the command deck lights, chin propped up on his right knee. The light of the consoles further catches his growing out bangs as Turiso continues to gaze out, his pose a clear display of boredom.

In the near distance, a family pod of 14 leviwhales, 10 adults and 4 calves, dip and glide through the vast cosmos.

Their soft blue bioluminescent forms like winged shuttles flying through the darkest depths of space, long fins spread out as they catch even the faintest of solar winds. Their bodies full and broad, heads long and narrow, powerful flukes powering them onwards towards their end destination. Thick hides protect them from the void of space and the pressures of the various atmospheres they encounter on their long migrations across the Artelaine Realm. The hides of the older adults more knobbled than that of the younger animals.

The matriarch of the pod is the largest, over 600 metres in length. Green streaks light up the lumps on her long narrow head as she guides her pod forward.

The pod remains undisturbed by the duo of starships tailing them as they move towards to their winter feeding grounds, some 5 systems away. The younger leviathans were initially enthralled with their new shadows, daring to get that little bit closer to them, but not once straying too far from their pod.

The leviwhales are unlike anything Turiso has ever seen. He knew the gentle giants were beautiful, but to see them with his own neon green eyes during the initial first days of this mission; it was truly awe inspiring.

Exactly how Turiso has grown bored of watching the leviwhales Kel has no idea!

Kel has always loved them.

Sure, undertaking this mission meant he couldn't be with his girls on Stellaris Day, but Jack did well to snag the mission in the first place and his ex-wife had made her plans well in advance.

Leviwhales have long been mysterious in nature. Creatures of ancient history dating back long before sentient races had mastered space travel, somehow they have managed to survive events that should have made them go extinct. Galactic war, hunting and viruses have tried and failed to entirely wipe them out.

At various points in their history, leviwhales could be found across the cosmos. But in the present day the species is typically only found in the Artelaine Realm, sometimes straying into the neighbouring Junas and Varmpas Realms, their numbers somewhere between 30,000 – 34,000 at best estimate.

Graceful Angel remains locked on her automated cruising course, keeping a lawful distance away from the cetaceans. Flying parallel on her starboard side is *Sweet Remedy*. Unlike her bigger sister, the smaller RPM Class starship keeps her distance manually; this down to Jack once again running a navigational array diagnostic.

Kel had to laugh when Jack told him the reason behind this latest tinkering session. Who knew that S.T.O.R.M Delta Echo would be the operative to fall furthest behind on compulsory starship upgrades!

Whilst both mission-proven starships are winged specification designs, navy blue as their primary hull colour, the similarities end there.

Graceful Angel dwarfs her slightly lighter hued station sister, her bulkier form less angular, neon silver cheatlines prominent on the contours of her hull. By her name sits her personal insignia; a winged flying woman based on the angeli of Atra; a peaceful lightspeed race who keep to themselves within the Evelon Realm.

In truth there isn't really much for the trio of S.T.O.R.M operatives to do, aside from observe the cosmic cetaceans and issue cautions to other commuters in the region.

Of which there have been none.

The mission itself is a welcome break for the trio during the traditionally hectic final month of the year. Yet Turiso finds himself wishing for action once more. He'd love to join Jack in her upgrades instead of being stuck on *Graceful Angel*. Kel has everything covered from the starboard science station, leaving little for him to do except watch for absent traffic.

"I can hear you thinking," Kel warns him.

Turiso startles at the sound!

"And no Jack wouldn't want you on *Sweet Remedy*," Kel states, "she would also warn you that bored is no state of mind for any S.T.O.R.M field operative, let alone a mercie. And trust me on this, you're safer here; Jack is creatively evil when it comes to bored field operatives."

"What do you suggest then?" Turiso asks in mild annoyance, spinning around in his seat, his annoyed gaze falling on his pack-mate and mentor.

S.T.O.R.M Sierra Tango is a living legend.

The hulking blue mohawked 6'5ft mercie is an honest veteran not just of S.T.O.R.M but life in general. To fellow operatives he is a good friend and listener.

To the galaxy he is a friendly face with an electric blue mohawk that is as striking as his chiselled physique. Kel's army of adoring fans would be immensely disappointed to learn their idol doesn't spend hours working out, rather his impressive stature is due to his genetics; a good majority of humans from Azari Nex share the well defined muscles trait.

Turiso counts his blessings for knowing Kel Williams. Even by his own admittance his S.T.O.R.M life so far has been rather stormy in nature; a rather poignant level 10 on The Ekaitza Scale for measuring storm severity. Having the reputation of S.T.O.R.M's worst ever trainee precedes him by miles. His controversial premature graduation from the S.T.O.R.M Academy resulted in uproar, with Kel's neck on the line for it.

Yet the veteran was proved right.

Turiso, for all his faults and arrogance, had the mercie spirit deep within him. In the field he has begun to emerge as the field operative Kel and Jack recognised; a roughly cut diamond amongst rocks. It hasn't been an easy journey for the youngster, yet somehow the former military cadet has proven everybody partially wrong.

The youngster fits the general description of the typical mercie: lithe, muscular and ready to go at all times. History out of the equation he is no different from any of the other younger mercies Eagle Station has.

That Kel and Turiso share the same fashion choices comes as no surprise. Without him realising it, Turiso's own on-starship attire mirrors that of his mentor's. Both of them always opt for tight fitting blue t-shirts that cling to them like second skins, their metal insignia pins attached on the left hand side above their call signs. Both opt to pair their t-shirts with colour matching utility trousers and knee high duty boots, decorated with eagle yellow trim to indicate them being mercies.

Kel's blue eyes are full of their usual warmth as he checks his monitors, a slightly bemused smile gracing his sculptured features as he carries on with his duties.

"Check the scanners, Bravo Victor. That's an order," Kel commands, still not looking up from his screen.

"Oh come on, Kel! I've checked the scanners loads of times! I know more about those leviwhales than I do about S.T.O.R.M's history! And that's really saying something seeing as you made me read a dozen books about S.T.O.R.M's history last week!" Turiso protests.

"Clean the command deck then, Turiso. Just do something constructive with your time," Kel suggests, pretending he didn't just give an command and get ignored.

"I did that 2 hours ago!" Turiso snaps.

The younger op throws his arms up in frustration. Kel tries to dampen down the rather inappropriate laugh threatening to erupt from his throat.

Taking Turiso under his wing has proven to be his best decision in a long time; the younger operative has a tendency to be unintentionally hilarious!

"I had noticed you've cleaned the deck, Bravo Victor," Kel acknowledges, "and well done on that task. *Graceful Angel's* command deck has never been this clean, and that is going up against Wynona's cleanmatic robots. But you need something to do; I can't have you sitting there saying 'I'm bored' every 5 hours or so."

The clyemnarian groans in protest.

"Have you fed the goldfish?" Kel offers.

"Fed them and nearly lost my fingers!"

This time Kel can't stop his laugh!

"It's not funny, Kel!" Turiso protests.

"I did warn you they bite!" Kel chuckles, finally looking up at the youngster.

"I thought you were joking!" the younger mercie exclaims, "they're bloodthirsty beasts!"

Kel roars with laughter!

Turiso's look of exasperation doesn't help.

Kel leans back, wiping a tear away from his right eye, chuckling as he brings himself back under control.

"Nope. Jack brought me those bad boys for my birthday last year. She did warn me they were the ballistic predatory kind, after I stuck my hand in the tank that is."

"And you still have fingers?" Turiso asks in disbelief, "I'm calling you out on that, Kel."

"Oh Jack fed them beforehand, she's not that psychotic, at least not yet she isn't," Kel reveals, wiping yet more tears out of his eyes, "sorry, she just neglected to mention to me that she'd fed them until after she played her prank. Was amongst her better pranks to be honest. At least it didn't involve flying cake."

"Flying cake? Whatever!"

Turiso rolls his eyes, moving his seat back and forth, feeling his sanity draining away.

"And because of this mission, those snappy buggars on *Graceful Angel*. I prefer them being in your quarters away from me," he complains.

"Language," Kel warns, "and it is only temporary. I'll move them back to my quarters once we get back to Eagle Station," Kel reiterates yet again.

"Good!"

Kel smirks at that.

Turiso's annoyed expression gives way to a rapid onset of confusion.

"Hang on a minute, flying cake?"

"Don't ask," Kel warns him, bursting back into hardcore laughter a second later.

Turiso's eye roll is justified.

The veteran field operative pranks are the antics of legend, especially the devious pranks of the Eagle Station veteran ops. During his time with Kel, Turiso has witnessed them first hand on a number of occasions.

Highly amusing?

Yes.

Scarily creative in application and design?

Usually.

Catch you off guard each time?

Especially when they concern a certain S.T.O.R.M Delta Echo on a revenge prank.

Killer goldfish, outer hull cement bombs, exploding cat-shaped pancakes, laughing gas and all the pranks that go down in Eagle Station's recreational area Go Sportivate.

Turiso still hasn't gotten over Jack's zombi mannequin leaping out of the main ball pit last month. So much for the place being an area of fun for the field operatives; over a dozen of them pulled out pistols and shot the unfortunate mannequin!

Turiso shudders at the memory of it.

When Jack threatened to get her rewind operative back for his superglued toilet trick on *Sweet Remedy*, Jack wasn't joking! Turiso might not know Erick all that well, but nobody deserved that heart attack in a ball pit!

"What do you suggest I do then, Kel?" Turiso ask in defeat, spinning back around in the pilot seat to stare back out into space.

"Give Jack a bell," Kel offers, "she must be close to finishing her diagnostic by now."

"She's probably found another of *Sweet Remedy's* systems to take apart *without* actually taking it apart," Turiso groans as he taps into the communications system.

"Ha! Now you're starting to understand her!" Kel praises, "keep this up and she might spare you for being bored."

"You're kidding me!"

"No I'm not," Kel promises in a sing-song voice, "I've told you before: there is no such thing as a bored field operative, especially when you are in close proximity to S.T.O.R.M Delta Echo."

"When did you mention that statement? No wait; cold time after that Natra mission when Jack wandered off. I remember asking you where she was going," Turiso remembers.

"To lay a trap for Erick as she had nothing else to do at that point," Kel adds, "and as such she wasn't bored. Instead she was living up to her impossible reputation by building a realistic looking console made out of chocolate cake. Erick actually fell for that prank too for an entire week, the daft buggar."

Turiso moans in despair as he spins around in his seat, tapping into communications via the silver console on his right.

"*Graceful Angel* to *Sweet Remedy*."

"Receiving you, what's Kel doing this time, Turiso?" Jack asks aloud.

"Looking at the scanners again," the rookie answers, looking over his shoulder, "like he's been doing for the past 3 hours."

"Why aren't you?" Jack questions.

"I'm piloting the starship."

"On automatic? Stop being bored and check the data," Jack orders of him, "there's a tonne of research to do."

"I've seen it loads of times!" he protests.

"So check the data again," Jack orders.

Kel chuckles his breath, shaking his head in amusement. He saw that coming a million miles off.

"I have checked it many times, Jack!" the clyemnarian reiterates.

"Check it again then."

"Jack, there is nothing new to do!"

"There is always something new to do."

Kel smirks as he hears a defeated groan of annoyance emit from Turiso.

"Turiso, check the data or I'm boarding your starship and kicking your arse. And Kel, why are you slacking with the kid? You're supposed to be setting the example, not leaving his arse kicking to me! Who am I? His mother?" Jack demands.

"Oh charming, says the mercie taking apart her starship for the hundredth time today!" Kel counters.

"I'm Delta Bloody Echo; if I don't do this I'm not living up to my meticulous reputation of almost being a gennie," she outlines.

"Meticulous reputation of being a planet-locked engineering geek, "Kel counters, "you make the Lantos design teams look like normal sentients."

"Bite me."

Kel laughs out loud.

"I'll take that win any day," Kel decrees with a grin, "plus knowing you've self-inflicted this."

"You just watch out," Jack warns coldly.

"Ha! So how we punishing Turiso for saying this mission is boring then? He's already cleaned the command deck and fed the killer goldfish," Kel asks her.

"Kel, you lazy buggar! Why is it the rookie's duty? They're your goldfish so you feed them!"

Kel laughs in disbelief.

"This coming from the person who dumped a galleon of fake blood in there to play a joke on Wynona once?" Kel challenges.

"It was your idea, Kel! You wanted to get her back for that salted coffee gag."

"What?!" Turiso asks in shock.

"Yeah, that didn't go down too well as a prank; it backfired on us quite spectacularly," Kel confesses.

"Backfired on you, I managed to blame Erick and escape on a mission," Jack corrects.

Turiso groans in protest.

"Shut it, Turiso," Jack commands.

"Jack Fact 21#," Kel indicates with a knowing nod, "Jack will always make you learn a lesson."

"Do I really have to learn the Jack Facts in full now?" Turiso asks in exasperation.

"No," both veterans answer in unison.

"Really?" Turiso replies, sobering up.

"Really. Now go back to studying those leviwhales, or else," Jack threatens.

"Okay op," Turiso agrees promptly.

"Jack would rather you didn't learn the Jack Facts," Kel indicates, "or rather she'd prefer it if you didn't turn into a Jack Fact spewing rookie. Trust me you would regret it, and I don't mean me kicking your blue uniformed bum regret it."

"He means you shoved in an airlock and threatened with death if you do turn into a fact spewer," Jack corrects.

"Right, well dodging that topic, I honestly thought this mission would be exciting. Y'know, save the leviwhales; be part of protecting them and ensuring their survival. I thought it would be action and adventure rather than just follow at a safe distance and take notes from the starship's scanners," Turiso complains loudly.

"And inform traffic to change their courses, providing them with new routes to avoid further trouble," Jack adds.

"But we haven't seen anybody since the start of the mission! And that unmanned space probe we saw doesn't count! It was a piece of derelict space junk!" Turiso protests.

"Bravo Victor, ever since your academy days you have been fully aware that this role isn't all about being a hero," Kel reprimands.

"I know that!"

"Ha!" Jack laughs.

"Act like you do then. You know the mission codes; worded and colour, well, in theory you should," Kel warns.

"Of course I know the codes! But whoever decided to call 'watch from a distance missions' research-pursuit missions obviously wanted to make it sound more exciting and dramatic than it actually is," Turiso argues.

Turiso regrets his words immediately.

Kel straightens up in his seat, his eyes turn colder, fingers drum on the edge of his console. The stern look of annoyed disappointment says exactly what Kel is thinking. Visibly Turiso shrinks in his seat as he spins around to face him.

"Okay, let's face facts here, Bravo Victor. We are studying a critically endangered species of spacial cetacean. Do you know just how many scientists and students would donate their organs to science to do what we're doing right now? To be out here in space, studying the leviwhales?"

"Hundreds?" the rookie offers.

"Try thousands, Turiso," Kel states, "literally thousands upon thousands."

"Don't forget the S.T.O.R.M ops who were pissed we got this assignment," Jack interjects, "it's only because I got in first that we landed this mission. Seriously this is our busiest month of the year and here we are not rushed off our feet."

"Slacking off," Turiso snorts.

Kel's unamused expression is Turiso's final clue not to push his luck.

"Just so you know, Turiso, pursuit in Zaraka means follow, and we are doing just that; following the leviwhales to research them. Jack did good to land us this mission. Hell both my girls wanted to tag along, but they're with their grandparents this year, and as for my son, well he's in the S.T.O.R.M Academy the old fashioned way, which means he can't skip out like you have."

"Not from lack of trying," Jack reminds him.

"Not from lack of trying indeed, I know, Jack, we both tried to get the rules bent a second time but failed," Kel replies.

"And the ungrateful rookie is bored."

The sunken malice in Jack's voice is a new tone to Turiso's all-hearing ears. Sure he has heard S.T.O.R.M Delta Echo annoyed a few times, especially after pranks played on her, but this tone is colder, darker than he's ever heard from her.

It sends a shiver down his spine.

"Okay first, I did not know that word meaning," Turiso admits, unable to look Kel in the eye any longer, even turning his head away from the built in ceiling speakers, "and erm, sorry. I didn't know about Giana and Natalie wanting to come on the mission, and wait, you have a son who is in the S.T.O.R.M Academy?"

"My oldest lad Rick; he's been in training for the past year and a half," Kel explains.

"Born the same year I started my training," Jack comments, "and I'm convinced he's going to become a para, Kel. He knows his medical stuff like I know my starship engineering."

"Oh he's set to become a mercie, Jack, you just watch," Kel promises with a smile, "he might know his medical stuff like a pro but he's still an all rounder. Not that it matters which branch he joins; I just want him to be happy and make his own decisions."

"You mentioned having 2 sons before now, Kel, what about your other son?" Turiso asks, curiosity getting the better of him as he faces Kel once more.

"Scott?" Kel replies, "he was accepted into The Tyerria Sporting Excellence Academy earlier this year, and good on him too. I'm glad he didn't feel pressured into joining S.T.O.R.M like his old man and big brother did," Kel praises.

"Future medallist," Jack points out, "he's training the distance for The Galactic Games."

"We'll see," Kel replies with a smile, "either way I'm proud of my boys for pursuing what they love."

"Well, I'm sorry for being ungrateful, Kel, and you too, Jack," Turiso apologises, "I guess you're both right about this mission and what it means."

"Apology accepted, Turiso. Now get back to viewing those scanners and do your duty," Kel orders.

"Okay op," Turiso agrees, turning around to resume his duties.

Kel smiles; Turiso has learnt his lesson.

"Jack, have you finished with taking apart *Sweet Remedy* or not?" Kel asks the other mild annoyance in his life.

"You're not funny," Jack warns him.

"Darling, I'm hilarious," Kel promises.

"Ha!"

Jack just knows her former pack-mate has winked at her; she doesn't need to see it.

"For now I think I'm done, give or take a second look at the secondary navigational relay switches," Jack confirms.

"Jack, *Sweet Remedy* has back ups of her back ups of her back ups, plus a relay that supports her back ups. I'm pretty sure it'd be impossible for your starship to die," Kel teases.

"That's the general idea, Sierra Tango."

Kel chuckles.

"You and that bloody starship, honestly! We need to get you a decent hobby that doesn't involve starships, blowing up cakes or pranking your call sign rewind excessively."

"No thank you," Jack politely declines.

"Ha!" Kel laughs in response, leaning back in his seat, "y'know, Jack, it's a shame that

Harmony isn't here. She would be loving this mission."

"I thought she was all action?" Turiso asks.

"You're kidding right? Harmony's a nature maniac. But Harmony is on that much needed sports break I managed to sort out. She's not missing on much," Jack dismisses.

"That was sweet of you to arrange that, and well scored too," Kel compliments.

He can hear Jack shrug it off.

"She needed the break," she states.

"Can't argue there," Kel agrees, "what's the latest on her old man?"

"Still in a coma, no change."

"Are her blood relatives still treating her like utter crap and Harmony still covering it up?"

"Of course they are and yes."

"Starhell demons," Kel curses.

"Harmony's got us; we're her real family," Jack counters, "and Harmony is gonna learn it either way or any."

Kel nods in agreement.

"What's your dad doing today anyway, Jack? You've neglected to tell me," Kel asks her, realising that conversation hadn't actually cropped up.

"Not another secret mission I hope! That's what he hinted at to wind me up."

Kel laughs out loud.

"He's supposed to be helping my brother from another mother with his archaeological stuff," Jack states.

"What's a secret mission?" Turiso asks her.

"Take a big calculated guess, Turiso," Kel offers enigmatically to his young charge.

"Strikeforce?" Turiso logically guesses, remaining focused on the consoles in front of him as he adjusts Graceful Angel's course slightly to port.

Much to the rookie mercie's surprise the veterans burst into a roar of hard laughter!

"Think more so inside the bedroom, Bravo Victor," Kel advises.

It takes a mere second...

"Oh gosh! No! Seriously?!" Turiso realises.

"Yep; Jack's had a decade of this. It's how her brother was born to be honest," Kel jokes.

"I heard that, Kel!" Jack yells, "besides, Robbie's not that much younger than me, and accidents happen!"

"Oh, your brother was an accident was he? I bet he loves you!" Kel teases her.

"You know what I mean Sierra Tagger!"

"Delta Belter!" Kel fires back.

"What is it with the insults between you guys? Honestly! Every single freaking time this happens when there's a lull in missions!" Turiso complains.

"Get used to it; things turn to jacksh-"

"Language, Delta Echo," Kel advises.

"As if your tongue is completely innocent," Jack counters, "if only your beloved fans knew what language flows so beautifully past that ragged tongue of yours."

Kel can hear her smirking, which he knows is never a good sign; a smirking Delta Echo is a scheming Delta Echo.

"Now you listen-"

"Yeah, Kel, you swear like a vikirian foot soldier on a good day," Turiso chips in.

Jack snorts in bemusement.

"You watch it, Bravo Victor," Kel warns, pointing a finger to the back of Turiso's seat, "you're in deep water going up against a duo of vets."

"You said the exact same thing to me back in the day and look what happened? Remind me, Kel, which smart cracking rookie showed you up a treat back in the day?" Jack pushes.

"I've spent every year since then trying to deal with her, sorry, I mean IT."

"Ouch, that joke went out of fashion 10 years ago, keep up with the times, Kel."

"So did your tinkering."

Turiso groans in final annoyance.

Just the cue Kel and Jack were waiting for.

"Okay I am done with you old timers! I'm using the bathroom then I'm going back to checking the datastream, if this is what you guys are going to do for the next hour!" Turiso snaps in defeat, storming off *Graceful Angel's* command deck in the process.

"Welcome to the Sierra Tango school of learning; enjoy your complimentary headaches and backwards lessons," Jack replies to the sound of heavy boots as the younger field operative thunders down the stairs to the accommodation deck.

"Get me a black coffee while you're down there, Turiso! Extra sweet!" Kel orders, smirking in bemusement at his pupil's actions.

As expected Kel gets no response.

Jack's impressed sounding whistle is loud over the open commlink.

"That worked," Kel comments.

"It did," Jack agrees, "he'll learn, Kel."

"He will," Kel replies, "give him his dues, he has come a long way in a rather short period of time. He'll be a top mercie once he has settled fully in his role. At least on missions he is mostly showing he is worthy of the mercie call sign; that medical outing to Cartago proved it."

"Have his music pursuits helped him settle down somewhat?" Jack asks.

"They have but I've got my duties cut out with him," Kel admits, his eyes returning to the data before him, "hang on a minute, Jack, it looks like the leviwhales have altered their course."

"I see it," Jack confirms.

"Turiso! Get your backside back up here!"

4. TURNING POINT

On the scanners Kel watches *Sweet Remedy* surge off on an intercept course. The sound of thundering boots up *Graceful Angel's* central staircase heralds Turiso's hurried return to her command deck.

"Station. Follow Rems," Kel orders.

"Okay op," Turiso acknowledges.

Returning to his seat, Turiso takes hold of the controls, surging the Discovery Class starship forward into rapid motion. The familiar reverberation of engines reaches Kel's feet as his girl follows after her mission sister. His eyes continue to study the data before him, the multicoloured display charting the unexpected movement of the leviwhale pod.

"Turiso, the leviwhales are on a collision course for the planet Torero," Kel informs the younger op, "we need to stop them."

"Okay op."

"We've got this," Jack assures them.

"That planet is kilerra class, Jack. If the leviwhales enter the atmosphere they're dead. Might not be toxic to them but they'll never navigate their way out of its atmosphere due to its dense magnetic fields and high energy electrical storms," Turiso acknowledges.

Kel is momentarily stunned by this!

"Somebody's been doing his homework," Jack notes as the duo of starships close on their targets.

"Told you I had," the clyemnarian retorts.

"Not now," Kel cautions, his eyes back on the numerous scans and route projections.

He doesn't like how this looks.

His monitor informs him both starships are flickering their external lights, using the same warning patterns the leviwhales use for communicating to each other about danger, Kel having activated the sequence on *Graceful Angel* with Jack doing the same on *Sweet Remedy*.

But rather than the leviwhales responding to them, the cetaceans are doing the opposite.

"They're speeding up," Kel declares.

"They must have misinterpreted the lights for something else," Jack guesses.

"Should we inform Raptor Station?" Turiso suggests to his fellow ops.

"Negative, Turiso. There's nothing they can do; it's down to us to save the cetaceans," Kel dismisses.

"What about the Val'Kii SAS?" Turiso asks.

"I've already sent them an emergency call but their nearest cruiser is 24 hours away, and that's if they can help us. In this instance we're the better equipped force to handle the situation," Jack states.

"So no back up then?" Kel concludes.

"No back up," Jack confirms.

"Buggar."

"The Val'Kii SAS doesn't have specialised gear for kilerra class planets. The Artelaine Rescue Corps does; they have atmosphere probes, but those would have to be modified, and even then they'd take a minimum of 48 hours to get here," Jack explains.

"Okay op," Kel acknowledges.

"Perhaps the leviwhales have confused the geomagnetic energy in the planet's atmosphere for something closer to home?" Turiso soundly guesses.

"Sounds legit to me," Jack concurs.

"Try increasing the light sensitivity by 30%," Kel advises, "that might help."

"Doxsi Dora," Jack confirms.

"Okay op," Turiso answers.

The bioluminescent glow of the leviwhales grows larger as the starships approach, closing the distance down to less than 100 metres. Alerts blare out from both starships. Angry red warnings declare proximity detection notices on the pilot displays for both starships.

"We're breaking the law today ops," Jack quips, "I hope The Unity forgives us."

"Well somebody's got to be the incredibly lawful criminals, Jack," Kel replies, "it might as well be a trio of S.T.O.R.M operatives."

"Not the first time S.T.O.R.M ops have been the galactic bad guys is it?" Jack replies, her bemusement apparent.

"True."

"Are you guys seriously discussing the Tyerria Repulsion right now?" Turiso demands as the duo of starships reduce their speed, moving within 50 metres of their rescuees.

"Actually no, I meant in general," Jack clarifies, "but the Tyerria Repulsion works too as an example."

Kel's eyes remain fixed on his screen as the lead leviwhale eyes up the closing spacecraft. The strange machines have been following her pod for some time, keeping their distance over the past 3 days. The gentle matriarch spreads her long fins wide, her body dipping and diving as she guides her pod to the safety of the strange new feeding ground ahead of them.

She doesn't know why the spacecraft have gone on the offensive after all this time, but she doesn't want to stay around to find out why. She flashes brightly to her pod to hurry up.

"What if we detonate low yield missiles in their path? Risky but that might scare them off course and save them?" Turiso suggests.

Kel immediately spots the downside.

"I don't see The Galactic Science Council agreeing with that when they find out. Jack?"

"Low yield starshatter missiles on radius burst. But make sure they are at least 600 metres ahead of our rescuees otherwise Sara is going to be kicking our arses," Jack advises.

"You mean The Galactic Science Council?" Turiso queries, "surely they'd be first?"

"No, Turiso. Our Operations Director would chew us up so much that The Galactic Science Council wouldn't get a look in," Jack explains.

"Ah."

"Lock and load, Bravo Victor."

"Selecting low yield starshatter missiles on radius burst," Turiso confirms as he punches in the weaponry commands into the red console on his left.

His eyes fleetingly glance over *Graceful Angel's* weaponry display, returning to the sight of the leviwhales. Turiso really doesn't want to do this but they're fast running out of options.

"Cetacean impact with upper atmosphere in 98 seconds," Kel announces, "we need to get a move on ops."

"Weapons locked on target," Jack confirms.

"Turiso?" Kel asks.

"Locking coordinates 650 metres ahead of the targets," the younger operative confirms, "ready to fire upon command."

"Okay op."

"Good thinking on the distance, Turiso, I'm aiming 600 metres ahead," Jack praises.

"Okay op."

"On your mark, Kel," Jack indicates.

"Standby," he advises.

With a quick check of the coordinates selected by both pilots, Kel double checks their hit areas.

"Go for rescue, open fire."

Both of them go for their red fire buttons.

Simultaneously twin streams of blue light flash out from the forward weapon ports of both starships.

They veer.

2 go starboard.

2 go port.

"Missiles away," Jack confirms.

"Impact 10 seconds," Kel acknowledges.

The slim matt black missiles race past the leviwhales at high speed, steering towards their explosion points.

Bright red sparks burst into life.

Green sparkles explode behind them.

The space between the leviwhales and the planet erupts into a rainbow of colour.

"They're turning about," Kel calls out, clocking the leviwhales movements on his monitor, "that's done it!"

"No it hasn't," Turiso counters.

"Buggar! You're right!" Kel realises with a check quick to the leviwhales positions, "they're going under the detonations. Those sneaky buggars! I thought leviwhales were afraid of bright explosions?"

"Wild animals, Kel," Jack reminds him, "good luck predicting their movements."

"Yeah yeah; they can react in any which way or any, right next plan then."

"Let's load another volley," Turiso states.

"Negative on that, Turiso. The leviwhales are in distress. If we do a second volley we'll might end up killing them," Jack objects.

"We can't just do nothing!" Turiso snaps, "how about we try to barricade their access to the planet instead?"

"The rookie's learning fast," Jack admires.

"They're speeding up again," Kel indicates.

"We see that," the pilots reply in unison.

Almost in sync the 2 incredible starships twist and twirl, their flight paths erratic, trying to divert their rescuees.

Sweet Remedy sweeps from starboard.

Graceful Angel sweeps from port.

The eyes of the frightened leviwhales follow the starships actions, the calves peeking out from the centre of the pod, watching as the strange spacecraft come to a halt directly in the path of their grandmother.

The lead leviwhale is having none of it.

With a bright white flash of her hide the leviathans disperse, effortlessly evading the alien spacecrafts, their paths still placing them on course for the planet.

"Buggar! What about charge deflectors? Bright, harmless, very distracting; they work against weapons, maybe they might just work to send the leviwhales off course?" Turiso offers.

"Good thinking," the veteran ops agree.

In unison *Sweet Remedy* and *Graceful Angel* accelerate away once again, overtaking their rescuees once again.

"Make it quick, we've only got 50 seconds left to save them," Kel warns them.

"Deploy charges," Jack announces.

"Okay op," Turiso acknowledges.

The space between the starships and the leviwhales lights up like a Stellaris Day firework display. Bright flashes of red, white, yellow and green burst into life! Through the blinding light however, the scanners tell no lies...

"Buggar to hell!" Kel curses loudly as as the leviwhales ease past their would be rescuers.

"There's nothing more we can do for them," Jack calmly replies, "atmosphere contact in 35 seconds and counting. We can't follow them in; our starships aren't designed to handle kilerra class planets. We'd only be dooming ourselves to oblivion if we tried it."

"We can improvise a way to follow them. There's got to be a way to protect our starships surely," Turiso assures his peers.

"Liking your thinking, rookie," Jack agrees.

"Oh boy it's a Jack Fact 9# mission again," Kel whistles, already punching up the Discovery Class schematics files, "Jack always does the impossible."

The duo of starships veer off, moving into geostationary orbits as the confused leviwhales disappear into the pink murk of Torero's maze-like atmosphere. Watching the final leviathan vanish, Jack can't help but wonder if they can actually pull this mission off.

In theory she knows *Sweet Remedy* can fly through a kilerra class planet's atmosphere; a breakfast bet with her call sign rewind 4 years ago saw her figure it out the old-fashioned way on paper, but actually putting that theory into working practise?

"Jack, this is usually the point you bust out Jack Fact 18#; as much as you hate the Jack Facts," Kel points out.

"Never insult *Sweet Remedy* within earshot of Jack - just don't. How is that relevant?" Turiso asks.

"That's 12#, Turiso, 18# is Jack always has a rough idea of what she's doing," Kel corrects, "right, Jack?"

"Right," she confirms, "I have a theory on how to pull this off, but I will stress it is just a theory. Bear with me, I need to put Rems into a secure geostationary orbit."

"Turiso."

"Already on it for *Graceful Angel*."

"*Sweet Remedy*, lock in a geostationary orbit over target coordinates," Kel hears Jack state over the commlink.

GEOSTATIONARY ORBIT CONFIMED.

"Let me guess, you figured out the theory over breakfast after somebody challenged you to do it," Kel guesses logically.

"Erick," Jack confirms.

"Huh? Here was me thinking it might have been Harmony who challenged you."

"She's a sports junkie, not suicidal, and engineering feats aren't her type of challenge."

"Good point. She just loves trying to give you heart attacks instead," Kel concedes.

"I didn't hear that."

Kel laughs out loud.

"Now, this theory is just that; a theory. I have no idea if this will actually work or not," Jack warns, "and it's only applicable to *Sweet Remedy*. I'm not sure if I can work it for *Graceful Angel*."

"I'll take a Delta Echo theory over anything; you always figure things out in a crisis," Kel counters.

"So do you," Jack objects.

Kel smiles.

"Nope, I am not taking the win for this; impossible missions are your speciality, Jack. They always have been."

A heavy pause fills the air.

"Right then," Jack replies, breaking the silence, "let's get to work on this. I've got digital copies of my files backed up."

"Okay op. Turiso, knowing Jack she's got the RPM Class sorted so that just leaves our girl to figure out," he states, turning to his packmate.

"Can't be that much different to figure out given my theory is based around reducing energy output to absolute minimum levels," Jack reasons from over the commlink.

"Actually I might be able to help here, Jack, I've been learning the ins and outs of Discovery Class systems," Turiso replies.

"Right let's see what you geniuses can come up with then," Kel challenges.

"Something worthy of the Jack Facts existing outside their original intended purpose," Jack declares, her eyes darting from their new rescue zone to *Sweet Remedy's* engineering station...

5. ECHO'S CALL

WARNING.
EMERGENCY POWER LEVELS AT 83%.
"Hang in there, Rems."

Jack's eyes momentarily fall on the commlink audio lines in the bottom right of her head up display. A trio of blue, yellow and red lines jitter to the sounds of the stormy planet. Nothing but static fills the crackling airways as the RPM Class speeds through the atmosphere climbing higher and higher.

"Another 1000 metres and we might be able to reach Kel," Jack assures both of them.

"*Hopefully.*"

A loud roar of thunder to starboard serves as a warning. Jack guides her starship to port, dodging a small sphere as she continues her spacewards climb to safety.

At least they tried.

1 hour and 5 seconds.

It's better than Jack could have hoped for.

Sweet Remedy has once again done the impossible; another notch in her long record of missions.

Steering to starboard whilst increasing her girl's speed, Jack can't help but notice a new pattern appear on the audio lines.

Sweet Remedy is quick to recognise it too.

Immediately the starship's pilot station computer taps into the rear science station, running an algorithm to check the new pattern for audio spikes.

Jack holds her course.

Could it be?

WARNING.

EMERGENCY POWER LEVELS AT 82%.

A lighting strike to starboard almost hits!

Jack goes evasive.

She dodges to port.

She dodges to starboard.

WARNING.

EMERGENCY POWER LEVELS AT 80%.

"Buggar!"

Sweet Remedy's screens briefly flicker out.

Jack's blue eyes go to the audio lines.

The regular sharp static spikes return.

"Nearly home, Rems, nearly home," she assures the battered starship as she channels additional power from the auxiliary weapon systems batteries. Why she didn't think of that sooner she hasn't a clue. A green command on her left side console indicates success.

"That should give you that 2% back."

TARGET IDENTIFIED.

"Wait, what?"

Jack's eyes go first to the giant sphere in their way then her readouts.

KABOOM!

If Jack hadn't blinked she would've sworn she'd missed something.

The readouts vanish.

Command deck lights flicker out.

Sweet Remedy's engines whine down.

Her controls stop responding.

Within the blink of an eye *Sweet Remedy's* systems are completely dead.

"Oh no."

Jack scrambles once again out of her seat.

A jolt throws her to the deck.

Desperately she scrambles and crawls to the engineering station, trying to reach the open console from earlier.

It's her only hope.

The hairs on the back of Jack's neck prickle. She snaps her head round to see her worst case scenario. As the starship's nose dips, dull grey consumes the view. The veteran field operative braces herself against the outer edge of the engineering station, shaking fingers spreading out.

The shaking and gusting stops.

The deck plating stops vibrating.

Delta Echo lets out a slow breath.

Stillness.

In the air a very slight tingling of charge hangs motionless. Jack's eyes remain fixated on the void outside.

It feels almost serene.

The deadly danger of the situation lost in hazard translation. For all the menace she has faced on this mission, all of it has evaporated.

Her starship feels weightless.

Even in space *Sweet Remedy* has a persistent weight; a comforting mass that feels solid and alive. When docked at her home base of Eagle Station, *Sweet Remedy* is alive to the hum of her computer core, her life support systems and whatever her operator is up to at any given time.

Sometimes music plays over her intercom as Jack tinkers away on a system upgrade or a project. Sometimes the infamous starship is alive to the sounds of nutritional destruction as Jack records an explosive cooking vlog. Other times the starship is alive to sound of Jack noisily supporting her favourite racing team as she watches The Galactic Championship, or plays digigames or any of the other 101 things she gets up to onboard her starship.

Then there are the times *Sweet Remedy* is running full pelt to a mission, her own sense of gravity present and calming. No matter what, the RPM Class is always doing something, always on the go, always noisy, always has a mass.

But now that motion, that spark of life that defines her, that spark has gone...

A thundering roar of wind brings her back.

Bright angry pink crashes into her!

Jack springs into action as *Sweet Remedy* flies back into the primary danger zone.

A loud bleep echoes out.

Neon light brightens the head up display.

The hum of engines greets Jack's ears.

Monitors and consoles return to life.

The pink, purple and blue dolphin-esque body of the Delphinus Galaxy fills the starboard side main monitor.

A hum reverberates through the deck.

Jack blinks twice as she looks over the pilot station consoles, praying she's living this for what it actually is.

SYSTEMS REBOOT COMPLETE.
ALL SYSTEMS GO.

"I'll damned to hell."

To her shock *Sweet Remedy* has fired back up on her own with no hassle!

"Okay, have it your way then, Rems," Jack agrees, leaping for her pilot seat and strapping herself back in.

She'll figure this out later once her starship is safely back to cruising the cosmos of the Artelaine Realm.

LEVIWHALES DETECTED.

"What? No way!"

Jack's eyes go to the audio lines.

They indicate only static.

Jack strains her senses to find their targets.

"*Sweet Remedy*, you're losing the plot," Jack declares after several seconds, "that's just increased static on the radio – wait, what's that?"

A loud echoing cry wails through the violent air, the audio lines erupt into a frenzy of activity.

"Holy power coils!"

LEVIWHALES DETECTED.

Jack hones in, using her well oiled hearing, *Sweet Remedy's* barely functioning systems and her own gut instinct.

LEVIWHALES LOCATED.
FLIGHT LEVEL 293.
DIRECTION NORTH EAST.
DISTANCE 590 METRES.

"Yes! Found you!" Jack shouts in elation.

Another long whining cry echoes from outside *Sweet Remedy's* hull as Jack swings her around, dodging a sphere to port and a second to starboard, the battered starship starts a steep climb.

LEVIWHALES LOCATED.
FLIGHT LEVEL 290.
DIRECTION NORTH.
DISTANCE 590 METRES.

Jack makes the course corrections.

Lightning flashes too close for her liking.

She grapples for control against the gusting winds, eyes going to her compass.

LEVIWHALES LOCATED.
FLIGHT LEVEL 291.
DIRECTION NORTH EAST.
DISTANCE 600 METRES.

"These guys are moving fast," she notes.

Thunder growls from not too far away as Jack guides *Sweet Remedy* around another sphere, realising her mistake only a fraction of a second too late.

Sweet Remedy shuts down immediately.

Luckily for Jack she reboots straight away.

Carefully she eases her girl onto the tail of their rescuees, using the foot controls to prompt more speed from *Sweet Remedy's* engines.

LEVIWHALES LOCATED.
FLIGHT LEVEL 289.
DIRECTION NORTH EAST.
DISTANCE 550 METRES.

"C'mon, come to Jack," she murmurs.

Jack looks to her altitude.

284.

284.

284.

"Buggar," Jack realises.

Sweet Remedy's altitude reader is stuck.

289.

The sudden leap would've caught a lesser pilot out, but not Jack, given she's seen this happen ever since the beginning of this rescue mission. She keeps going, dodging the spheres of doom, battling the gusts, her senses focused on the dual task of surviving and rescuing.

LEVIWHALES LOCATED.
FLIGHT LEVEL 289.
DIRECTION NORTH EAST.
DISTANCE 459 METRES.

The distance is finally closing.

Over the static echoes of familiar wails intermix with the constant static. Faintly Jack smells a metallic tang in the air. *Sweet Remedy* is going to need a full overhaul before her outing from Eagle Station.

LEVIWHALES LOCATED.

FLIGHT LEVEL 290.
DIRECTION NORTH EAST.
DISTANCE 400 METRES.

In the distance, vague alien shapes start to emerge from the gloom. Jack watches in awe as vague shape become familiar pale blue bioluminescent hides, glowing gently amongst the angry storm clouds.

"Hello leviwhales," she greets with a smile.

Sweet Remedy counts 14 leviwhales in total; Jack breathes a sigh of relief.

"Even the babies are still alive."

LEVIWHALES LOCATED.
FLIGHT LEVEL 291.
DIRECTION NORTH EAST.
DISTANCE 370 METRES.

Jack hits a switch to her right, starting up the leviwhale vocal recording she has on speed activation.

"C'mon, come to me, come to me, turn to me," she urges, turning her starship towards them, trying to follow their erratic course.

Over the roar of the wind and thunder Jack isn't sure if the leviwhales can hear her or not, but she can only hope they spot her somehow. Surely if she can see them, they can see her.

KABOOM!

"Oh buggar not again!" she curses as her starship once more dies of a lightning strike.

Sweet Remedy's nose dips sharply.

She lurches to port.

KABOOM!

The second hit is a direct hit to her port wing. The once again stricken starship pitches violently to port starting a fatal death spiral to the ground.

This time Jack knows she can't win.

She accepts it.

Fear claws at the back of her mind.

So much for being 'as fearless as a tauros shark' as a glossy magazine once described her. Jack snorts in amusement at the odd memory. Right now she'd give anything to be out of this deadly atmospheric maze.

Bracing the controls as tightly as she can, S.T.O.R.M Delta Echo tries to manually steer *Sweet Remedy* from going inverted. In the sight of a rapid flurry of scenery, she closes her eyes, focusing on the motions of her trusty starship, using feel alone to guide her to their inevitable demise. A loud rapid clicking sound draws Jack's audio attention.

BANG!

Jack's eyes snap open.

"What that, Rems?"

Sweet Remedy's nose levels.

Her systems remain inactive yet somehow the starship has levelled up, her death fall forgotten.

Jack gawks in shock.

"I don't believe it," she mutters.

Leaning over the top of her consoles, a soft blue glow greets Jack's vision; a very familiar soft blue glow that illuminates the bottom half of

Sweet Remedy's head up display. Jack's eyes look up as a shadow passes above.

"Incredible!" she gasps.

Another of the gentle leviathans appears to starboard, calling out in a long wail.

Another leviwhale appears.

And another.

And another.

Then the largest of the calves followed by his mother and an aunt.

Jack has no words for what she is seeing.

All of the leviwhales reach for space above, their wing-like fins spread wide, their powerful ocean blue and amber flukes powering them and their wounded rescuer to freedom.

Jack is 89% certain *Sweet Remedy* is on the back of the lead leviwhale judging by the echoes and squeaks she feels and hears reverberating through the hull. She has seen many sights over her long career yet this is amongst the most eerie and beautiful of all.

This is another level of encounter!

Like so many others she has heard many stories of leviwhales approaching spacecrafts and astronauts out of curiosity, but saving a S.T.O.R.M starship?

The whole situation feels bizarre to the veteran field operative as the leviwhales pass a large grey sphere with ease. All the trouble she has had trying to pilot her way around yet the leviwhales aren't hassled in the slightest, cruising through the atmosphere effortlessly.

Below her Jack feels the rise and falls of her rescuer as they cut a path through the clouds, dodging the grey spheres of doom with natural skill.

"This is unbelievable! You guys are making this look way too easy! I have been fighting with the controls from the get go to find you lot! And yet, wow, I wish I had your skills around here!" she exclaims.

She leans back in her seat, taking in the view all around her. Now they've been found apparently the ex rescuees are able to perfectly guide themselves to safety.

All Jack can do is watch.

Higher and higher they climb through the tempest, space beckoning to them like a calling card. Jack knows the leviwhales are highly intelligent creatures, making a calculated guess that the leviwhales have put 2 and 2 together and realised she has come after them to save them. The veteran operative has no idea that she is spot on with her guess.

The pod's own veteran leader soon realised she'd made a mistake. The planet she thought to be an unexpected rest stop was no feeding ground for them. Yet the geomagnetic signature was so similar to that of their normal feeding grounds a mistake was always going to happen.

The signature was a trap.

A strange eerie echo that looped over and over as they searched for an exit in the pink never ending maze. The sight of the strange spacecraft that tried to stop them earlier is their surprise salvation.

Some of the adults have seen the likes of the blue spacecraft before. Normally they come in peace; the matriarch thought that was wrong earlier when they opened fire. She knows now she was in the wrong for doubting the spacecraft and her larger friend.

They knew the dangers here.

They tried to stop them.

Now this spacecraft is in danger too, no doubt from trying to find them in this alien place.

She has to save it.

She has to return the favour.

As the leviwhales continue on their way up Jack watches in wonder at the giants around her.

Their movements fast for their size.

Their communication rapid.

Their bioluminescent flashes lighting up *Sweet Remedy's* command deck.

Jack has observed leviwhales many times before, but this is something else, something beyond. The field operative part of her brain snaps her out of her awe induced daze.

Blue eyes go to monitors and numbers, taping in commands on consoles. Jack takes a calculated guess of their ascent rate and starts to prep for reboot. In theory *Sweet Remedy's* main power core should reboot automatically upon detecting space.

The theory part has Jack worried.

Her starship has taken more damage that she anticipated, spent way longer in Torero's atmosphere than Jack originally calculated. The veteran starship has done her role above and beyond, but whether or not she will actually spring back to life after spending so long on emergency power, and being hit by lightning, is another question.

Jack can only hope.

Sweet Remedy must reboot.

"C'mon, Rems, don't let me down."

The clicks between the leviwhales become quicker and more high-pitched.

The ascent angle steepens.

Higher and higher they climb.

Space beckons like a beacon.

To starboard the youngest of the calves dips into view, craning her head around to look at the little flying thing currently on her grandmother's back. A series of clicks from an unseen leviwhale snaps her head around to focus on where she is heading instead.

An idea pops into Jack's brain.

From a compartment to her left Jack retrieves her trusty wrist computer W.O.C.U.S, tapping its touchscreen as she slips the electric blue and gold trimmed gauntlet onto her wrist. Immediately the Wrist Operated Computerised Utility Supporter's screen lights up a bright amber, S.T.O.R.M's colourful insignia displays on its homepage.

Jack selects the audio recorder speaker symbol, the black and silver audio player activates, giving her a multitude of options.

She selects the bright red record button.

Immediately the device starts recording the beautiful theme song resonating around and through the starship.

The roars of thunder.

The whistles of the wind.

The crackles of lightning.

The vocalisations of the leviwhales.

The soundtrack of this mission.

Jack puts her hands back on *Sweet Remedy's* controls. She has no way to tell how far they are from space, yet oddly that doesn't concern her as the leviwhales effortlessly turn away from a sphere on their course, twisting to starboard then port to resume their course.

A particularly loud whistle echoes through the command deck.

"I see them," Jack assures her rescuers.

6. HEROES

A smile graces her features.

Through the murky turmoil of vibrant pink, a dark shade of black starts to emerge, stars scattered across it. Like a dense fog lifting pink gives way to black.

Storms give way to stars.

Static gives way to silence.

Spheres give way to the vast cosmos of the Artelaine Realm in all its splendour, the navy blue hull of *Sweet Remedy* reflecting the neon blue glow of her rescuers. Before Jack even has a chance to think about the manual fire up procedures, *Sweet Remedy* reboots.

Lights flicker into life.

Engines hum strong and proud.

Air whooshes as it starts to circulate once more around the command deck, doing away with the climbing humidity. The ceiling lights strengthen in intensity as main power returns, bathing *Sweet Remedy's* command deck in white light. The metallic texture of her ceiling and pearlescent sheen of her navy blue and eagle yellow interior revealed once more in all its splendour. The primary screen displaying the Delphinus Galaxy glows that little bit brighter, the S.T.O.R.M insignia appearing in the bottom right corner, its trio of stars sparkling.

**MAIN POWER RESTORED.
ALL SYSTEMS GO.**

"Yes!"

Jack breathes a sigh of relief, laughing as she relaxes into her seat, a finger gracing her W.O.C.U.S to end its vocal recording of the incredible leviathans.

She wipes a hand across her face, feeling the cool blessed air lick at her sweaty t-shirt. In the heat of the mission she never realised just how warm it had truly gotten.

On her head up display Jack spots *Sweet Remedy* pick up where W.O.C.U.S has left off, a blue audio line indicating her starship has automatically synced to the wrist device and is continuing the recording.

A loud series of rapid bleeps emits from the ceiling speakers, prompting Jack to involuntarily jump in her seat.

**SAFETY MODE DEACTIVATED.
STARSHIP: RPM *SWEET REMEDY*.
OPERATOR: S.T.O.R.M DELTA ECHO.
FULL SYSTEMS ACTIVATED.
CAUTION. HULL DAMAGE DETECTED.
SYSTEM DIAGNOSTIC REQUIRED.**

"Run it, and set an autocourse to follow the leviwhales as per galactic law standards," Jack confirms.

COURSE CALCULATED.

Jack double-checks it via her navigation console to her right, ready to confirm the course selection.

Movement catches Jack's left eye.

She looks up.

Her eyes go wide in awe to the sight of a lone female leviwhale heading back towards her, the gentle giant's fins spread wide as she glides through the vacuum of space.

Sweet Remedy's command deck bathes in bioluminescent blue as the creature glides closer and closer towards, finally coming to a halt, a meter away.

The large female turns, her deep blue eye falling on the small figure within the spacecraft, a large fin reaching forward to rest gently on the starship's hull.

Rescuee and rescuer meet eye to eye.

Sentient to sentient.

Blue eye to blue eyes.

For what feels like an eternity Jack feels locked in connection, reading deep into what the leviwhale is saying, what she is feeling.

Gratitude.

Respect.

Curiosity.

Relief.

Humility.

A low pitch rumble echoes through *Sweet Remedy's* hull, through her operator and out into space. With a gentle wave of a fin and flick of her flukes the contact is lost.

Jack blinks.

It was only for the briefest of seconds, yet the deep swallowing blue of the leviwhale's eye captures the veteran's mind. She lets out a slow breath she didn't realise she was holding, her eyes watching as the older mammal returns to her pod, dipping and diving through the cold vastness of space.

"We've got your back," Jack murmurs.

On scanners Jack clocks *Sweet Remedy's* larger mission sister flanking to port on a parallel course.

A bleeping alerts Jack to an incoming call.

On the head up display the message illuminates in right in place of the audio lines. The familiar starship insignia of a encircled winged female fighter giving away the identity of whom is calling her.

It prompts Jack to smile.

"*Graceful Angel* to *Sweet Remedy*, Jack, are you alright? And by alright I mean not sporting any serious big bruises or concussions or infected eye injuries," Kel's voice rings out across the open air commlink.

Jack laughs out loud, finally confirming *Sweet Remedy's* autocourse to follow the leviwhales on their new course to familiar feeding grounds.

"Seriously! What was that mission?" Turiso shouts over the commlink, "you guys keep hinting at this mission! It's not even funny anymore dammit!"

"Language!" Jack and Kel snap in unison.

The admonishment stuns all of them into silence, giving way to an awkward pause.

"I hate it when we do that," Jack confesses, with only *Sweet Remedy* to hear her.

"I'll tell you later if you don't say 'I'm bored' for more than 5 hours," Kel promises Turiso over the comm.

"Like I haven't heard that before!"

Jack chuckles as she accepts the call.

"Love you too, Kel. I found the leviwhales and no nasty eye injuries this time," Jack replies cheerfully.

"Jack!" Turiso complains.

"Regular call out. I got stuck up a fake tree after being chased by killer catfish," Jack explains badly,

"What?! But that makes even less sense!"

The consoles before her eyes go fuzzy, forcing Jack to shake her head clear.

"Concussion. Fantastic."

"We'll tell you the full details later, Turiso. I promise. We can see that you found our rescuees, Jack, but I asked if you were alright not if you'd repeated your greatest past hit mistake," Kel reiterates.

"Argh!"

"Shut up, Turiso, watch the leviwhales."

Jack snorts with laughter.

"Couldn't be better," she answers happily.

"Yeah, not falling for that jack-"

"Language, Sierra Tango. By the way, Turiso, seeing as I'm feeling generous, that mission we keep alluding to?"

"Don't tell him," Kel interjects.

"I'm telling him. We've both tormented him enough with this," Jack counters, "basically, Turiso, on a regular call out, once upon a time, a long time ago, things went unregular. I ended up in a swamp, killed a skyrider by accident, or 'winged a skyrider' as you've heard Kel say, got stuck in the mud, stuck in a swamp, came face to face with giant crocodiles and a large killer catfish, swam for my life, escaped via a overhanging fake tree and I ended up with a black eye and an eye infection for my good intentions, amongst other minor injuries. Lucky I had my W.O.C.U.S on; it saved my wrist."

"That's crazy!" Turiso exclaims.

"That's normal."

"That's only half of it. That regular call out is a nightmare even on a good day," Kel admits.

"Especially on a good day," Jack corrects.

"Well if you're going to tell him the story you might as well tell him the third half of it," Kel scoffs.

"I'm getting to it, Kel," Jack promises, "wait, shouldn't that be third third? Never mind. The following mission I got shot in the same eye by a blaster."

"So it was 2 missions then?"

"Yeah, basically."

"Wow, talk about unlucky."

"If I got a bottle of whiskey for every time somebody said that," Jack seethes, "I wouldn't be able to pilot *Sweet Remedy* from being completed rat-arsed."

"Jack, you feeling okay? Just that you love flying your girl," Kel asks her teasingly.

"Yeah, I'm fine, just stating the obvious as per Jack Fact 3#, as much as it pains me to say it," she dismisses.

"She really winged that skyrider in the first mission, Turiso. We had to get a new one to replace it," Kel replies.

"Don't blame me for that error; a crocodile tried to eat me!" Jack reminds him.

"Wait, so crocodiles, killer catfish, fake trees. What happened in the first third? Vicious dogs?" Turiso guesses flippantly.

"Actually you're right there, well guessed."

The groan of disbelief is loud on Jack's hearing, but it still prompts her to smirk.

"As if I would blame you, Jack. I remember your call whilst you were shooting at that crocodile. Now shut up and tell me how big your bruises are, S.T.O.R.M Delta Echo. I've heard your voice waver," Kel orders.

"She sounds fine," Turiso argues.

"No, Turiso. It's only slight but it's Jack's tell that she's taken a hearty hit, and I don't mean to her ego," Kel corrects him.

"Small, now stop trying to parent me, Sierra Tango. Honestly, you dad me worse than my actual dad."

"Cute, Jack, how old are you?" Kel asks.

"Old enough."

"Wait, what did Jack just say?" Turiso asks in complete bafflement.

"Basically she said 'Kel, shut the hell up because you're worrying too much'," the older veteran translates.

"Again," Jack adds.

"Again. Basically it's a Delta Echo version of saying shut up," Kel explains further.

"How does that even translate to shut up?" Turiso asks him, sounding even more confused.

Jack smirks, trying her hardest not to laugh. On the inside she does feel a bit sorry for the younger operative, but not sorry enough.

"It doesn't, you just accept it makes sense and leave it at that," Kel confesses.

"Great," Jack hears the youngster mutter.

"This isn't over yet, Jack, I'm coming aboard *Sweet Remedy* to check you over."

"No you're not! I'm fine!"

"Put your W.O.C.U.S on then and set it to transmit your biosign."

"I'm already wearing my W.O.C.U.S," Jack grumbles as she activates it, tapping for the field op bio settings.

"There," she offers after a few seconds.

"Thank you, Delta Echo."

The comms fall silent as Kel runs over the fresh readings. Jack herself clocking the multicolour readout of her physical state. A number of bruises and the concussion Jack had already clocked but dismissed. *Sweet Remedy* is in worse shape than she is.

"Concussion looks mild, but you know the drill, Jack. Any symptoms?"

"Some vision blurring earlier but nothing I can't handle. And that's not me being stubborn-dismissive, Kel; I feel alright generally. And yes I'll deal with it."

"I know you will. Use a neuralwave and that will fix that. Call me if you need me."

Jack snorts in disbelief.

"As if. You'll be watching the readouts like a hawk until the Val'Kii SAS get here."

"True," Kel agrees, "but you absolute mad paddleslapper of a delta belter, you bloody well did it didn't you? You found them! Nice effort, Jack!" Kel praises proudly.

"Ha! Well it was only a case of protecting the core. Any RPM Class operator would've figured it out eventually. Hell, I bet if you'd have asked our Talia, she'd have told you within 20 seconds what to do," Jack dismisses.

"I've just seen what our Sahara Jeroshi has put on the S.T.O.R.M Forums and she says you're completely mad! That only a maverick as mad as Delta Echo would attempt something so damned risky," Kel reveals.

"Oh you haven't put this on the forums already? For a love of Tyerria, Kel! Come on man! Seriously? Buggar to hell!"

The laughter is way too loud for Jack's tastes as she buries her face in her hands, leaning back in her seat.

"Cheer up, Jack, I was only updating fellow ops and the mission. You know how jealous they are," Kel teases her.

"By the way, India Juliet thinks you're mad too," Turiso adds, "but she's used to it."

"That is a terrible joke coming from her," Jack replies, voice muffled by her hands, "I swear she's trying to give me a heart attack."

Daring to look out into space again, she drops her hands, shaking her head in relieved annoyance.

"She's worse than I am! Seriously, who willingly goes canoeing in a crocodile infested swamp for a sports outing? At least I crashed a skyrider because I was trying to stay alive!" Jack replies, transferring her comms to her W.O.C.U.S.

"I know! I said that too," Turiso replies, "well, not the staying alive part. I only just found that out."

Jack frowns as she stands up, resting a hand on the seat's yellow headrest.

"Bravo Victor, please tell me you haven't told S.T.O.R.M India Juliet that she's a mad op who is worse than me. Just please, tell me you haven't," the veteran all but begs of him.

"Why?" the younger mercie asks her.

"Because only an utter idiot winds up Harmony Alonso. Even I don't do it and she's my pack-mate," Jack points out.

Turiso laughs out loud in response.

"Jack's right y'know, Turiso. Harmony will eat you alive if you have said that to her, and don't forget that it's Jack she's best friends with on call," Kel warns the youngster.

"Leave me out of this; Harmony's pranks are a different level of insanity compared to mine!" Jack protests, "getting the neuralwave now, Kel."

"15 minutes minimum," Kel advises.

"Doxsi Dora."

"Oh please guys! I can handle India Juliet," Turiso dismisses nonchalantly, laughing it off.

Jack and Kel both gulp in worry to the younger op's declaration.

"That's what Echo Delta said before he ended up cemented to a toilet seat with thermocrete after being sneak-fed Talak hot peppers," Jack points out, "he learnt the flaming way."

"I'm smarter than your rewind, Jack, I know what I'm doing," Turiso scoffs.

"Oh I'm telling Erick you said that!" Jack promises, "you think my mannequin in the big ball pit was bad? Don't try him, Turiso, or you will be sorry. That said, Harmony is going to get you back and I am not covering your back when she does, and her last prank involved a reprogrammed skyrider so you're doomed."

Jack pauses, eyes going to her engineering station as the cogs of her mind click.

"I have a modified neuralwave under that station thinking about it."

"Jack," Kel warns her.

"It's the one you gave me, Kel!" she snaps.

"Okay, okay, sorry," he replies in response to Jack's snarl of annoyance, "and Turiso paying for his crimes against ops aside, everybody admires us, especially you, Jack, for being your usual fruitcake self," Kel praises.

"Jack Fact 17#, right?" Turiso checks.

"And here was me about to say Turiso helped me with the design application for the mission," Jack snarkily replies, stalking towards her engineering station.

"Not anymore?" Kel offers.

"Oh I am taking full credit for this mission, especially as my girl was the starship to actually find the leviwhales," Jack boasts in retaliation, reaching for a securely locked storage area underneath the engineering station's main desk, "thank you Harmony for suggesting I put it here."

Removing a small silver first aid pouch, Jack makes quick work of the zips, removing the soft, malleable silver disc from the pouch. Only just smaller than Jack's palm, she presses the flexible black touchscreen on its surface. Soft blue readings spring into life as Jack presses the disc to her right temple.

"It's on."

"I can see. Right, don't worry about the readings, I'll keep tabs on you," Kel reassures her.

"Thanks, Kel."

"Anytime little sister, anytime. Just make yourself comfy in your pilot seat for now and chill. You can start patching up *Sweet Remedy* later."

"What about *Graceful Angel*?"

"Oh she'll live," Kel dismisses, "Turiso's already made a start on some of the repairs."

"Good lad," Jack compliments as she takes to her pilot seat once again.

"For now. Turiso is still getting his arse kicked later. Besides you're always going to be the hero in the eyes of everybody," Kel points out, knowing full well it isn't in Jack's nature to be egotistical.

If anything Kel knows Jack will try not to take the credit for the mission win, or at the very least downplay her role in it, resulting in Jack's usual ear bashing on the S.T.O.R.M Forums about her trying to downplay her achievements.

Jack snorts in amusement.

"Great, more hero worship I didn't order."

"Nothing new there then," Kel reminds her.

"Ha! That!" Jack laughs heartedly.

"Hey, Kel, we're getting a call via a private commlink," Turiso informs his older pack-mate.

"Take it downstairs," Kel advises.

"Okay op."

"Bottle of 2390 Tiger Whiskey says that's Harmony," Jack bets as she hears Turiso leave *Graceful Angel's* command deck.

Kel laughs.

"Nah. Loser scrubs the power conduits on both starships for a week," Kel counter bets.

"You're on, Kel! Got it."

Their conversation falls silent as they gaze out across the billions of stars stretching the cosmos. It never grows old to look upon, especially when in their foreground are beasts of incredible legend. Without knowing it the duo of veterans both lean back in their respective pilot seats, eyes gazing to the leviwhales pod and beyond, simply taking in the view of the space beyond and before.

"Well this puts Torero on the tourism map," Jack concedes as she stands up, heading over to her engineering station to begin her damage assessment.

"Yeah. Well done there!" Kel agrees.

"Well done to you. *Graceful Angel* went first remember, Kel. Don't forget the first part of the mission."

"But *Sweet Remedy* went the distance."

"Team effort, Kel," Jack reiterates.

"Do you know how long you were in there for all told, Jack?" Kel asks her.

Jack glances to the engineering monitor to her immediate left. The tap of commands Jack inputs into the console controls is audible over to commlink to her good friend.

"According to Rems, we were in there for 1 hour, 15 minutes and 48 seconds, wow! That's way longer than I guessed."

"Exactly, you didn't just do the impossible, Jack, you set a brand new benchmark for the RPM Class – again I'll add. Well done, Jack!" Kel praises highly, "right, do I need to come over or are you going to behave for once and relax?"

Jack sits down in the engineering station seat, ignoring the intruding squeak as she leans back, drumming her fingers on the consoles.

Kel knows what that means.

"Jack. Talk to me."

Jack's eyes immediately find the floor of *Sweet Remedy's* command deck, noting some dust building up around the pilot area once again. She adds it to her list of things she needs to sort out.

"Jack. Start talking. I know when your mind is working overtime on something."

"Did you think I'd crash?" Jack asks him.

The soft chuckle says it all.

"No. Because you're the toughest buggar in S.T.O.R.M's history and if there is something you seriously major in, it is impossible rescues and scenarios. You always win when the odds are beyond reason," Kel explains.

"You're wrong," Jack corrects.

"Buggar! I shouldn't have said that aloud!"

"Miko would disagree with you, Jack. If anything he'd clip your ear for saying that. Now the important question, how's *Sweet Remedy* looking? Normally by this point you're gushing over your girl somewhat horrendously and have confused me with Jack techno-babble, so how is she?" Kel asks in concern.

"Bite me like a killer goldfish," she taunts.

"Ha! Now what's the damage?"

"Check your scanners, Sierra Tango," Jack bluntly replies.

"Delta Echo, I'm asking you because you're not following the post-rescue drama script and I don't see a medical reason for it."

Jack rolls her eyes in mild exasperation.

"She's still together," the blond operative deadpans sarcastically.

"Very funny. I can see that."

"So why did you ask then?"

"Because you always state the obvious and it's hilarious when you do."

Jack frowns in the direction of Kel's voice.

"I have never understood your sense of humour, Kel," she admits.

Jack's brain quickly clocks something.

It should've clocked this sooner.

"Stop playing me, Kel!" she warns.

The howl of laughter over the commlink is too loud for Jack's dented ego. She should have seen a mile off that Kel was deliberately winding her up with a sight joke.

"Alright, fine! Rems needs a lot of TLC given her damn safety mode kicked back into life randomly. She's got hull damage which I can't repair here, most of her secondary, tertiary and extra back up systems are done for, and I need to blow up a pancake or something for stress therapy," Jack accurately reports.

"See? Wasn't that hard was it, Jack?" Kel teases, "now let's continue with your feelings."

"Feed your fingers to your goldfish."

"Ha! Turiso fed them remember?"

"Buggar!" Jack curses loudly.

Kel's laughter catches.

Jack finds herself laughing along to their typical banter, a little annoyed Kel has tripped her up again, yet she wouldn't have it any other way.

"We done for now?" she asks.

"Never," Kel promises.

"I thought you might say that," Jack replies with a smirk.

"Well, Happy Stellaris Day, Jack."

"Happy Stellaris Day, Kel."

Faintly the sound of cursing echoes over the open commlink, followed by what sounds like to the veterans a garbled apology of sorts.

"That's Harmony on the line, you owe me, Kel!" Jack warns.

"Oh come on! No way is that Harmony on the line. She's on holiday for crying out loud!"

"And where does she upload her videos first, Kel? Because she doesn't send them straight to her S.T.O.R.M Connect account; she puts them on the S.T.O.R.M Forums first. That's Harmony on the line and you know it," Jack replies with a smirk.

"We'll see," Kel cautions her.

7. MOVING ON

"*Sweet Remedy* to *Graceful Angel*."

"Go ahead, Jack," Turiso answers.

"Time check 4 hours, go wake Kel up from his beauty nap," Jack orders.

"Any suggestions on how to do that?"

"Casually mention I've blown up a pancake; that should wake him up within a microsecond," Jack advises as she finishes off a diagnostic on *Sweet Remedy* from her pilot station.

"Why is that not a surprise?" Turiso asks.

"Because you're on Team Sierra Tango and you're getting used to his way of doing things," Jack surmises.

"Yeah. Say, Jack, mind if I ask a question?"

"You just did," she points out.

"Wait, Kel warned me; Jack Fact 9#?"

"Nope, that's I always do the impossible. Jack Fact 3# is that I always state the obvious," she corrects whilst checking a scan from *Sweet Remedy's* pilot seat, "and I do; it's a bad habit. A really bad habit actually, if I'm being honest."

"Right, I'm committing to learning these so I can taunt other rookies with them in the future."

"Don't you bloody dare," Delta Echo all but snarls at him, "I know for a fact Kel set you up to say that."

Turiso bursts out laughing.

"Dammit," Jack mutters under her breath, throwing her blue datapad down in defeat.

"Sorry, Jack, I had to make the joke at least once; Kel's orders," he apologises.

"It better stay at once," Jack threatens.

"It will! It will!" Turiso promises, sounding sincere over the commlink, "but I have to ask, who started the Jack Facts and why?"

"I started them as a joke; it escalated," Jack bluntly explains, "and then I arrested Rakellan Marius and the Jack Facts blew up in my face."

"Wow, sucks to be you then."

Jack smirks at that response.

"That's a good way to put it for half of the time, yes, sucks to be me indeed," she agrees.

"So how's *Sweet Remedy* looking now?" Turiso asks, doing his best to change the topic.

"She's looking better than she did earlier. I've managed to patch up a few of her injuries from the inside, plus I've had a chat with the RPM Class designer. She's going to have a look into new shielding for the class."

"Great!"

"She's also going to have a look at the Discovery Class, see if she can do anything there also," Jack adds.

"I can send her our readings," Turiso offers.

"Good thinking," Jack praises, "so go on, tell me, who called earlier?"

The question is obsolete but needed.

Jack already knows.

"India Juliet. Jack, I'm afraid."

"Ha! Kel owes me!" the veteran boasts.

Turiso groans in heavy despair.

"I'm doomed," Turiso glumly replies.

"We warned you," the veteran sings to him.

"I know, I know, I just didn't listen, and now I have to deal with whatever India Juliet has planned for me when we get back. Beats me why she's checking the S.T.O.R.M Forums in the first place."

Jack smirks.

"Harmony probably uploaded some vlogs or something. She loves sharing her sports antics as soon as possible," she explains.

"Well some of us are doing actual research. I've spent the last couple of hours charting the progress of the leviwhales. It turns out that the different aged leviwhales have different cruising velocities, however it is the lead leviwhale who determines the average pace the pod travels at," the younger op reports.

"I hope you're making notes of this to send out in your write ups later," Jack points out.

"Done something better than that; I've sent my findings to The Galactic Science Council along with your W.O.C.U.S recording," Turiso replies proudly.

"Nice thinking," Jack compliments.

"Thank you."

Jack leans back in her pilot seat, swivelling around to eye the mess of engineering tools now littering *Sweet Remedy's* command deck. She yawns, raising her right hand to cover it.

"Tired, Jack?" Turiso asks her.

"Yeah, kinda."

"Long mission," Turiso states.

Jack snorts in response, a smirk playing on her lips as she spots the small black spanner she couldn't find earlier lurking underneath the engineering station.

"Long year more like," she counters, "2395 has dragged on like a long haul inter-realm cargo hauler."

"Really? I think it's gone quickly," Turiso replies in surprise, "like really quick."

"The years always seem longer in the field. Wait until you've done a full year, Turiso. A year for a field op feels like a decade sometimes, especially if it's a bad year," she explains to him.

"Has 2395 been a bad year, bar me?"

"You just needed direction of a different nature; that doesn't count even in the slightest. And you've done good, Turiso. You've turned yourself around and shown you're a perfect fit for S.T.O.R.M, especially as a mercie," Jack clarifies.

"Thanks, Jack, that means a lot."

Jack doesn't need to see his smile to know it is there, the relief and gratitude in his voice is all too evident.

"2395 has been a good year for S.T.O.R.M. Y'know we haven't lost a single operative in the field this year?"

"Seriously?"

"Seriously."

"Wow."

"The average is between 4 – 6 per year."

"I didn't know that," Turiso admits.

"Death happens," Jack remarks, picking at some imaginary dirt from underneath her fingernails.

"Agreed there."

She smiles sadly.

"So next year will probably feel like a couple of decades then," Turiso guesses, "with the anniversaries no doubt you'll be kept busy with proceedings."

"I don't mind the anniversary stuff to be honest, Turiso," Jack admits, swivelling back around in her pilot seat, "the galaxy needs to remember the Tyerria Repulsion, and it isn't every year you celebrate 450 years, so it's not the end of Tyerria. Plus I'm the only op holding an original call sign at present."

"I guess so."

"Hey, that's my line," Jack teases.

"Sorry," the younger mercie apologises.

Jack chuckles in response.

"Say, Jack," Turiso states, "mind if I ask you that question now?"

"Shoot," she accepts.

"I just wanted to know something. What was Kel like when you and he were pack-mates back in the day?" Turiso asks her in interest.

Jack is a bit taken back. The question shouldn't come as a surprise given Turiso is

Kel's present pack-mate. It is only natural for him to be curious, but the question still catches her off guard.

Most accept Jack and Kel's friendship at face value without pushing deeper. Former pack-mates often remain close friends, even if they move to different realms or retire.

Sure Jack and Kel both pilot starships of their own, but Jack has lost count of how many missions they've run together, how many times *Graceful Angel* and *Sweet Remedy* has been mission sisters.

"Kel was a veteran even when I joined; his type always are," Jack explains, "he's amongst those ops who have seen field life before S.T.O.R.M and survived it somehow, but not without getting their share of battle scars."

"He's former Azanian Army, right?" Turiso asks in clarification.

"Yeah, that's right, he was an orphan; meant he had to join the military regardless and at a lowly rank. That force has always treated its soldiers as fodder, which is what Kel was before he eventually joined S.T.O.R.M," Jack explains to him, "when myself and Wynona joined S.T.O.R.M, Kel had already been an operative for a number of years. Him and Midnight were renowned as operatives."

"Wow, so it wasn't just you and Kel then?"

The surprise in Turiso's voice is abundantly clear. Clearly this is a conversation the duo are yet to have. In a way Jack feels sort of privileged speaking on her best friend's behalf to his latest pack-mate.

"There were 5 of us in total; Kel, myself, Wynona, a vikirian mercie called Midnight who was our leader, and there was also a younger male vikirian named Miko," Jack recalls.

"Is Midnight the blonde female vikirian in the photos Kel has in *Graceful Angel's* lounge?"

"That's her. She and Kel were best of friends, brilliant ops together and yes, Kel has always been kind; a bit of wind up merchant at times, but we all are, or rather we all end up becoming that."

Jack pauses, leaning forward in her seat. She rubs her chin as she thinks back over her long memories of living the pack life, prompting her to smile.

"Kel is the type to always have your back, even when you don't realise it. You can fight him, go on the offensive, but he'll always bring you home. What he does goes beyond duty and fieldwork, even friendship. He cares more than anybody else I've ever met. He never gives up and always has faith, no matter what. I might be the operative with the impossible reputation but the Kel's the operative with the sixth sense. He always knows when somebody needs him, and he makes sure he is there."

"Like with me?"

"Like with you, Turiso," Jack confirms, "he also has this weird tingle sense as we call it; he always knows when a mission is going to end with somebody seriously hurt; it's rather helpful actually," Jack reveals further.

"Kel told me he joined S.T.O.R.M in 2364," Turiso informs her.

"Sounds about right, I joined in 2375."

"So 20 years this year?"

"That's right; 20 years in the field."

"That's impressive. Wait, you're only in your thirties, Jack. That's kind of young for a human, isn't it?" Turiso asks in confusion.

Jack chuckles at that.

"Old enough to learn the role and to join the field, Turiso. Some grow up faster than others."

"I see."

"True I was on the younger end of the age bracket, but that did not detract from the fact I could do the field operative role. Some kids have more wisdom that adults twice their age. Take myself, I grew up with S.T.O.R.M, knew the ins and outs of it kinda like you with the Clyemnarian Marines."

"Wow."

"Well S.T.O.R.M brats make for easy to train field operatives. They always without fail go on to become strong in the field. Me? Well I lived up to that. I guess you could also say S.T.O.R.M is the family business for me. You've met my Dad, spoken with my younger cousin Syd on the S.T.O.R.M Forums. There's also an uncle on my mum's side who retired a couple of years ago."

"Mercie?"

"No, a para; S.T.O.R.M Deka Hawker. He operated out of Kittiwake Station on the Skarmonia – Evelon border. He might come back as an instructor I reckon, he gets bored too easily. And there's a few other family members in S.T.O.R.M too."

"What about your mother?" Turiso asks.

"Died when I was very young, that's how me and Dad joined S.T.O.R.M, because of what happened," Jack answers honestly.

In the distance she watches the leviwhales cruising towards their true destination, clocking the neon blue ETA for the approaching Val'Kii SAS cruisers on her head up display. The ships won't join them for another 2 hours at least, if they don't get called elsewhere.

"I see, so the rescued becomes the rescuer? Returning the favour and finding the rescuing to their liking?" Turiso guesses.

"Pretty much," Jack concludes, "and that's how Wynona and me ended up meeting Kel and Midnight."

"Have you ever fallen out with Kel?"

"Several times," Jack admits, "the biggest falling out we had saw us not speaking to each other for over a year. It took us a while to rebuild our friendship after that."

"I can't imagine that."

Jack chuckles.

"Anything can happen."

"So like any family you have your falling outs and arguments?"

"Contrary to the reputation I'm not perfect, Turiso," Jack points out, "none of us are, and after a particularly nasty mission a few years ago I wasn't okay. I tried to hide it. Kel thought he was acting in my best interests, but he wasn't. I returned the favour by breaking his office door down, getting into a fist fight with him and shooting him in the chest with a pistol on stun."

"Ouch."

"I was lost after that mission; an operative without a cause and Kel made things worse by acting without having been there."

"What mission was it? Code white?"

"The Sera Taisha mission."

Jack can sense Turiso's confusion over the commlink with ease.

"Sera Taisha? I've never heard of that mission, Jack," Turiso confesses, the veteran picking up on him shrugging his shoulders.

"Doubt you would have, it happened during a period us vets don't really talk about. But the files are out there if you fancy a read of them."

"What was it?" Turiso asks innocently.

After a brief pause Jack decides to tell him.

"The mission was a swampy code white evac-rescue call turned code sapphire."

"Death of a S.T.O.R.M field operative."

Jack nods in acknowledgement.

"Death of a S.T.O.R.M field operative."

"Has Jack finished patching her starship up yet?" Kel hollers up the staircase.

"And the conversation just went downhill in an epic death spiral," Jack deadpans.

"Confirmed," Turiso agrees.

Jack smirks at that.

At the same time Jack counts her blessings for Kel's timing; she really didn't want to tell Turiso the full story.

"What's she blown up this time?" Kel asks.

"A pancake shaped like your face."

"Ouch. 2/10 for creative endeavour, Jack."

"Bite me field operative on power conduit scrubbing duty," Jack counters, "for both starships I'll add."

"Oh you're kidding me! It was Harmony?" Kel groans over the commlink to Jack's elated laughter.

"What?" Turiso asks in confusion.

"Tell you later, Turiso," Kel promises, "very cute, Jack, now what's the latest modification to your starship?"

"Charming, Sierra Tango," Turiso and Jack reply in unison, both drumming their fingers on their respective piloting stations.

"Oh great, don't you paddleslappers team up on me again!" Kel complains, feeling a sharp headache beginning to set in.

"You prompted it," Jack states.

"Yeah well don't make this a habit, Jack. You have so many bad habits that S.T.O.R.M needs its next wave of field operatives to be cleaner than an ICU ward," Kel taunts.

"That was uncalled for," Jack objects.

"True though," Kel presses.

"Probably," she concedes immediately.

"Surely Jack's cooking vlogs can be called occupational therapy instead of a bad habit? She does help sentients to laugh and smile," Turiso offers.

Jack winces at the defence.

She can sense Kel's mood sour over the commlink, trying her best to stop a loud snort of laughter from escaping her nose.

"Jack doesn't need defending, she needs a year long cooking course plus hard exams," Kel points out.

"Hey! Come on, Kel, you know I'm a good cook; it's just that I absolutely refuse to admit to that on camera," Jack retorts teasingly.

"Alright I'll give you that; you do know how to cook without things exploding like fireworks," Kel concedes, "now tell me how *Sweet Remedy* is looking," he orders.

"Exactly the same as when you last looked out a window," is Jack's taunting reply.

Kel rolls his eyes again.

"Jack," he warns, "don't make me use my call-rank-on-you voice."

"I've done all I can for Rems without inspecting her hull from the outside. At present I've stopped for something to eat and to have a brief break."

"Did you find out what caused her safety mode to randomly activate?" Kel asks her.

"In theory, yes. In reality, no."

"Ouch."

"I've put it down to the weather," Jack admits, "seriously I've run every diagnostic I can think of, Kel. Even done a few checks that aren't in the manual and I still can't trace what the hell happened. With all the chaos she faced the weather is the only variable I can't actually test, not without actually flying *Sweet Remedy* back through the atmosphere at full power."

"Yeah, that's not happening," Kel states.

"No it isn't, but my girl's alright now so that's the main thing. I am tempted to take her back to Lantos, let Lynn give her the once over to be absolutely sure. Remember that safety mode issue *Soaring Heights* faced back in '92?"

"That was a kid who caused that, Jack. That said, there isn't much difference I guess."

Jack winces at the joke.

"Yeah I walked right into that jab," she mutters, clearing her throat immediately after, "my point being safety mode activating mid-flight is a never event; something that cannot happen; yet it has happened – twice."

"I'm sure that Eagle Station can manage without you for a week, Jack. Lynn would probably try to order you to Lantos anyway," Kel teases her.

"This is serious, Kel," Jack points out.

"I know, but I also know you and Lynn don't always get along very well."

Jack laughs.

"She loves me really."

She doesn't need to see Kel's grin to know it is splattered across his face.

"There's that too," Jack concedes.

"Either way it's another intriguing chapter in *Sweet Remedy's* long service career, Jack," Turiso praises, "she truly is a grand veteran of S.T.O.R.M's fleet."

"Excuse me, Bravo Victor?" Kel interjects, "our girl is older than Jack's and both of them have more years to clock if they want to start breaking records."

"Pull your trousers up, Sierra Tango, that's an order," Jack replies, rolling her eyes in mild bemusement.

"Yes ma'am," he cheekily replies.

"Hmm!" Jack huffs in good humour.

"You guys are so confusing at times, well a lot of the time!" Turiso complains to them.

"We know," the veterans reply in unison.

"By the way I'm filming a cooking vlog for S.T.O.R.M Connect later on, figured I might as well do something traditionally festive today," Jack reveals.

"Is it pointless for me to advise, 'don't blow anything up, especially the sweet things'?"

"Yep."

"And don't make a mess?"

"Yep."

"And to leave the pancakes alone?"

"Yep."

"Thought so; just remember to get a decent amount of rest. You went into hell and it'll be me facing additional hell if you don't take it easy. I'm supposed to watch out for you remember."

"Doxsi Dora, Fake Dad."

"Wait, Jack, why do you say that?" Turiso asks her in confusion.

"What? Fake dad? I'm winding Kel up."

"No you're not," Kel interjects.

"No! Doxsi Dora? Why not use 'okay op' like the rest of us?" Turiso asks in confusion.

Kel laughs out loud to Turiso's surprise.

Jack just rolls her eyes, shaking her head.

"Battlefield City; it's what her favourite character says and everybody has given up getting her to use 'okay op'," Kel explains to him.

"I can explain myself, Kel!" Jack protests.

"I know," Kel replies sounding all to pleased with himself, "but it is a perfect opportunity to wind you up some more."

"The stars damn you, Kel," Jack curses, though her voice lacks any anger as she stares into the distance to watch the leviwhales, taking in the pleasant sight.

Torero is almost a distant memory.

Much to the relief of all 3 operatives, the leviwhales headed on a course out of Torero's system, heading for open space towards their true feeding grounds. At a safe distance the duo of S.T.O.R.M starships continue their original mission; shadowing the leviathans, charting their progress across the cosmos.

"Beautiful aren't they?"

"What? Pancakes before you mercilessly destroy them for the sake of brutally explosive entertainment?"

"No! The leviwhales you paddleslapper!"

Kel roars with laughter!

"Oh those creatures! You should have said that, Jack, I completely misunderstood you," he teases her.

"No you didn't," Jack grumbles.

"How are you guys even friends?" Turiso asks the pair of them in exasperation.

The veterans snort in unison.

"From putting up with each other's bad habits since we first met," Kel explains.

"He's right," Jack concedes, "hey have you had to deal with Kel's stinky socks yet, Turiso?" Jack asks the rookie.

"You asked me that last week and the answer was yes!" the irritated reply states.

"Just testing," Jack teases, "Kel's socks can cause severe brain damage in field ops. You need to be really careful when dealing with them."

"Oi!"

Jack laughs out loud.

On her heads up display Jack clocks a blue comms light, a series of loud chirps make themselves heard across *Sweet Remedy's* command deck and her comm system.

"Galactic Centre to *Sweet Remedy*. This is Dala calling Jack. Delta Echo please respond immediately. This is a code white situation."

8. DELTA ECHO

"Dala!" Jack exclaims in utter surprise, straightening up in her seat.

"Wait, Dala? Who is she?" Turiso asks.

"Seriously?" Jack asks in annoyance, "you don't know who Dala is?"

"Chief of Galactic Centre. For her to call instead of a responder, something big must be going on," Kel explains quickly.

Jack taps to accept the commlink her end.

"Go ahead, Dala," Jack answers.

"I have a code white distress call coming in from a research cruiser that has been researching the Stellaris Comet. They've lost navigation and are on a collision course. *Sweet Remedy* and *Graceful Angel* are the closest starships we can pull from active missions," the long serving technician informs them.

"There's seriously nobody closer than us?" Turiso all but demands of the elder S.T.O.R.M member.

"Turiso, show respect," Kel warns.

"All available operatives in the Artelaine Realm have been despatched on a code white evac-rescue mission to Encore," Dala explains to them, "the Artelaine Rescue Corps have asked us to cover this; they've got their hands full with other emergencies."

"Dala, we've got the Val'Kii SAS due to join us. What about them, Jack? How far away are they?" Kel asks.

"Approaching from a different sector, we're closer than they are," Jack confirms.

"Jack's going, Dala," Kel informs her.

"Jack?" Dala asks in confirmation.

"Go for rescue," Jack affirms.

"I'll send you all the information we have, Jack," Dala informs her, "we haven't got much to go on but once you're underway I'll brief you further."

"Okay, Dala. Doxsi Dora."

On her display a fresh message pops up in yellow, indicating an attached information pack. As Dala ends the call, Jack opens the pack whilst setting in a course for the famous comet. Easily from memory she recalls the precise trajectory of the Stellaris Comet, using the info and coordinates shown in the received information to plan *Sweet Remedy's* route.

"No rest for the mercies," she quips.

"Sounds about right," Kel agrees, "are you going to be okay for this mission?"

"Yeah, I think so. If *Sweet Remedy* can handle Torero, she can easily handle the Stellaris Comet. It's only a chunk of ice and rock hurtling through the galaxy after all," Jack replies, focusing on her course calculations as she types them in.

"What about her hull damage?" Kel asks.

"I'll be careful," Jack dismisses.

"I don't care how well you know that comet, you be extra bloody careful, we need you back remember, Jack, " Kel cautions.

"I know, I know. S.T.O.R.M needs a poster op to keep the press happy whilst reminding Sara to get some rest," Jack replies.

"Actually I was thinking more along the lines of I need my best friend back to keep India Juliet off my case," Kel honestly states.

"Kel, don't bust your W.O.C.U.S. This is a simple save the spaceship mission," Jack indicates, "I've flown how many of these now?"

"You're flying into a comet; be careful," Kel warns, "remember what happened to *Swift Arrow* 3 months ago when Talia flew her into the Tate Comet?"

"Talia faced variables nobody could have anticipated with a comet that not many have studied. This is the Stellaris Comet we're talking about, Kel, and it's not exactly *Sweet Remedy's* first encounter with the thing," Jack dismisses.

"What could go wrong then?" Turiso asks them without thinking.

The veteran ops faces drop like stones.

The rookie senses he's done wrong.

"Buggar."

"Turiso, I swear if you have just haxed me I will hide your corpse somewhere where nobody in S.T.O.R.M will ever find it!" Jack threatens.

"You won't get chance; I'll murder the little buggar before that," Kel interjects.

"Ah. Mercie code?" Turiso asks.

"MY code," Kel deadpans.

"I get it! Don't say things like that! Wait hang on. What about Jack Fact 11#? I thought you weren't superstitious?" Turiso questions, "or have I got that wrong?"

"You got it wrong," Kel confirms.

"Jack Fact 23#, except for that particular statement, there's been too many patterns for my liking," Jack corrects.

"It goes without saying be on your guard on this mission, Jack. Your life is worth more than any other field operative," Kel reiterates.

"I will and I'll be back before you know it," Jack promises, "seriously, this is simple."

"You better be. We need to save Turiso from your pack sister," Kel critically declares.

"Oh Harmony can have him, Kel. I am not stopping her on this occasion, not after the metal wrap prank on Erick."

"Thanks, Jack," Turiso groans.

"You're welcome," Jack replies cheerfully, "keep me apprised on how things go with the leviwhales."

"Okay op. Good luck."

"Doxsi Dora."

With a final look to the gentle leviwhales and a tap of a blue confirmation to her right, Jack pulls back of *Sweet Remedy's* controls. The battered RPM Class surges to life, banking hard to starboard towards her next mission. Jack clocks the distance gained as her trusty starship accelerates away.

Her left hand goes to the throttle controls for lightspeed sitting low on their own lowered light blue console. A trio of silver levers primarily control lightspeed, with several small black switches controlling different settings.

A loud bleep accompanied by a green confirmation on the head up display indicates *Sweet Remedy* is in clear space.

"Go rescue time," Jack declares.

Her hand pushes forward the central lever.

It clicks into place.

RATE 1 SELECTED.
LIGHTSPEED THRESHOLD IMMIMENT.

As the stars turn to rainbow streaks, Jack smiles. A brilliant rainbow starburst explodes around the starship. Space streaks into a swirling rainbow tunnel of incredible colours, intermixing with white and silver streaks.

Jack's fingers move to the left lever.

She throttles up, accelerating the RPM Class to rate 5. The colourful rainbow effect of lightspeed accelerates too. Feeling her starship manage with the rate she accelerates again, taking her up to rate 8.

Jack taps for communications.

"*Sweet Remedy* to Galactic Centre."

"Go ahead, Jack."

"On course for the Stellaris Comet, present speed rate 8 on course 3947.8 to Spaceway 56. ETA to Junction 5 is 25 minutes. Full ETA to Rewna is 1.34 hours, barring any delays or complications; my starship has prior damage."

"SW56 is clear of traffic, you shouldn't have any trouble with it. I will put out a priority travel warning out just to be safe. Your starship damage has been noted. Bear with me 3 minutes and I will have fresh information on the spacecraft design you'll be dealing with. Maintain open commlink," Dala informs her.

"Thank you, Dala."

Switching *Sweet Remedy* over to automatic flight, Jack eases back in her seat, letting her mind wander over events of years past.

She can't deny that part of her is giddy with excitement of being able to see the comet once more. Even now she finds it slightly funny how a chunk of ice and rock can prompt so much festivity in the galaxy, but some festive days have sillier origins. At least with the history of celebrating Stellaris Day there is an actual solid reason.

The ancient people of the galaxy's oldest planet Rewna thought all life in the galaxy was going to die after a sunstorm erupted into life. The annual passing of the Stellaris Comet served as a post disaster reminder that all was still spinning.

Jack enjoys being on call on Stellaris Day.

For S.T.O.R.M, it tends to be a busy day across all the 12 realms of the galaxy, from the far reach of the Skarmonia Realm all the way across Evelon, Rus, Talak, Junas, the central realm of Artelaine, Varmpas, Del, S.T.O.R.M's home realm Lempra, Quai, Remida and finally the distant Olosol Realm; the 12 realms making up the Delphinus Galaxy.

Jack's smile grows as she clocks the date.

24th Kittapela 2395.

The Stellaris Comet will be right on top of Rewna. The planet has long since been uninhabited, save for the tourism season and archaeological digs, yet its impact on the galaxy at large remains.

The galactic standard clock.

The galactic months and days.

The early efforts of astronomers.

Then along came The Unforgiving War which all but turned Rewna into a dust ball in space. Jack makes a mental note to pull up the Rewna and Stellaris Comet files. *Sweet Remedy* herself has an extensive amount of data on both thanks to her multiple visits over the years.

The Delphinus Galaxy has a lot of history, S.T.O.R.M being part of its more recent. Even still it is incredible to think S.T.O.R.M is soon to turn 450 years old. Jack believes it; she's been nonstop doing PR things for books, shows and documentaries this year, all to be produced for circulation next year!

S.T.O.R.M is about to become the flavour of the year, and better yet, as the current holder of the Delta Echo call sign, Jack just knows that her schedule is going to be incredible!

Yet she wouldn't have it any other way, even though she'll never let that slip to the rest of her organisation. Jack is honoured to hold the illustrious call sign, its history dating back to the original 12 S.T.O.R.M field operatives.

The original holder; Tori Reed, went on to form S.T.O.R.M Medical, allowing the paras to become a thing. The second Delta Echo, Nova Yarada, played a vital role in saving S.T.O.R.M during their darkest hours. The third Delta Echo, Amoria Chanhia, held the call sign longest of all; 49 years in the field and then 20 as an instructor.

If only Jack could emulate them all.

From a storage compartment beneath the left-side consoles, Jack removes a much loved photo from a protective transparent case, the photo's edges now creased with age.

Down a deck in *Sweet Remedy's* lounge area, Jack has the same photo on a large canvas, hanging over her blue sofa. It looks almost identical to the sofa in the photo, except the photo sofa is occupied by 5 lively mercies.

Jack smiles fondly as she gazes upon the laughing faces. Kel looks exactly the same; his electric blue mohawk the same as Jack has always recalled him to have it. His physique impressive, showing beneath an electric blue muscle tank top, S.T.O.R.M written in big white letters across the front of it. His muscles flex as he leans into the shot.

Their female vikirian pack-mate Midnight Hunt has her arm around him, her long ash-blonde hair done up in a braided high-tail hairstyle. Midnight's sub-dermal ridged bone structures above her ice white eyes and around her wrists easily give her species identity away, her attire similar to what Jack wears in the present day.

Sat cross-legged by her feet is Jack herself, her long hair braided in a similar fashion to Midnight's. In the past Jack forever lived in turquoise blue t-shirts with the insignia emblazoned in the centre, pairing them with the standard electric blue utility trousers.

She used to prefer the lighter t-shirt shades back in the day when she was a young rookie, turquoise being her favourite colour. Over the years she drifted away from it, opting instead for electric and navy blues with yellow accents instead.

Beside Kel on the sofa are the sprawled squabbling heap of Wynona Sorbonne and Miko Ashington, the human and vikirian caught mid-laughter with Miko in a headlock. Wynona looked so young back then with her short brunette bob complimenting her green eyes, her attire all navy blue, a long sleeved t-shirt covering up the slavery scars on her arms, her Alpha Lima call sign written in small yellow font on the left hand side, her utility trousers the same style as Jack's.

After the pack broke up Wynona joined Jack on her newly appointed starship; the brand new RPM Class *Sweet Remedy*, 6th starship of her class and first of her class to arrive at Eagle

Station. Jack remembers that day like it was yesterday, smirking at the memory of it.

Flash forward to the present day and their lives couldn't be anymore different. Jack and Kel both field veterans, Wynona the chief of Eagle Station and second in command of S.T.O.R.M, Midnight long since retired, now a grandmother with her twin granddaughters starting their own training in the S.T.O.R.M Academy.

And then there is Miko.

The tanned vikirian who was the loveable joker of their pack with additional ridges on his hands and fingers Midnight didn't have. Jack knows these to be a regional thing to vikirians from the southern hemisphere of their original homeworld Rhagnai. Miko's attire is a lighter take on Kel's; just another way Miko used to wind Kel up, though Wynona and Jack were the usual targets of his jokes, Wynona more often in defence of Jack.

"Don't pick on the kid you brat!" as Kel used to reprimand him.

Jack laughs out loud at the memory.

"Oh, Miko," she sighs.

Miko was forever causing trouble, forever doing something to make them all laugh. Nobody was safe from the prankster, not even Midnight and she was pack leader.

Jack's eyes linger on Miko's face.

Like all vikirians his features are sharp and chiselled. He was tall too; he towered over

Wynona and herself. At 6'2 he was a bit shorter than Kel but taller than Midnight. What he didn't have in bulk he made up for in speed and stamina. It always proved useful on missions where they got bonus cardio.

Jack's smile wavers slightly as she averts her gaze to the rainbow tunnel of lightspeed travel. If only she could see Miko's dark blue eyes once more. If only he was alive and joining Jack on missions still.

27th Aratha 2377 was when the special photo was taken, on the long since retired Rapid Class *Soaring Wing*, captured forever by a millie who joined them for a short code blue mission to investigate a backwater planet.

The mission itself turned out to be a dud.

The 'strange signals' they were sent to investigate turned out to be a derelict satellite that survived a bumpy re-entry to begin transmitting old A-Pop songs again, albeit via a weak signal. The long return home however proved entertaining! This was when the photo was taken, on route back to Eagle Station.

What Jack would give to have the old pack back together again, even for just a few hours. Selfish thoughts but surely she's entitled to them as much as the next sentient along. Even heroes are just flesh and blood; something she isn't allowed to forget by those who know her for who she is, not just by her call sign.

Beneath the call sign is a young human.

Her eyes go to the photo again.

No, she doesn't want to go back to dodge the responsibilities of her life; she just wants to see Miko's smile again, hear his jokes, go on a mission that doesn't end.

But Jack knows the rules.

All of them.

Especially the first.

The first rule of rescuing is that you don't rescue everybody. No matter how painful it gets, the fact is not even the best S.T.O.R.M field operative can save everybody all of the time.

Death is inevitable.

A set milestone in life.

"10 years next year. It should be you out here saving lives, Miko, not me. It should have been me who died on Sera Taisha."

"Jack, you there?" Dala asks her.

The photo slips back under the console.

Jack wipes away a stray tear that has fallen from her right eye, clears her mind of emotion.

"Mind on the moment; time and a place."

"Go ahead, Dala," Jack acknowledges.

It's time for S.T.O.R.M Delta Echo to be the galaxy's favourite hero once again.

THE END.

"WE'VE GOT YOUR BACK."

GALACTIC BACKGROUND

*The following information has been abridged from The Unity Historical Records Library and The Galactic Library.

The Galaxy At Large

The Delphinus Galaxy is a remarkable cosmos. Located within a cluster of 40 other galaxies, the Delphinus Galaxy is a Masaoiua class galaxy which contains an estimated 120 – 160 billion stars. It is around 90,000 light-years across at present and comprised of 12 sectors, known as realms.

The 12 realms are:

1. Skarmonia
2. Evelon
3. Rus
4. Talak
5. Junas
6. Artelaine
7. Varmpas
8. Del
9. Lempra
10. Remida
11. Quai
12. Olosol

Named after rew astronomer Ava Delphinus, it is unknown when exactly Ava Delphinus was alive due to archaic files being lost during The Unforgiving War, however it is widely believed she was the first sentient to observe our galaxy and identity its dolphin-esque shape.

Rich and diverse with sentient species, the Delphinus Galaxy contains many inhabited solar systems. It has no fewer than 600 known solar systems, but it is estimated there may be as many as 1000 more as yet undiscovered.

Amongst its galactic neighbours it is regarded as the loudest due to the intense galactic travel of various sentients across the galaxy, helped in part by the network of inter-spacial spaceways, set up across all 12 of the realms.

The Galaxy Dating System

A Standard Galactic Year is made up of 12 months. Each month is broken down into 33 days as it takes Rewna a total of 396 days to complete a loop of its sun, Zaptra.

The 12 months were charted by a group of rew called The Sisterhood of Kalreene during ancient times on the planet Rewna.

The sisters studied their planet's cosmic movements in relation to a theory of relative spacial time.

These months are:

1. Karnao
2. Yyenn
3. Uollayn
4. Das
5. Serath
6. Aratha
7. Qwentas
8. Jawe
9. Manas
10. Repaba
11. Quoistas
12. Kittapela

The galactic months deprive their names from the defunct Rewna language Khe. They denote distinctive star constellations that were first observed above Rewna's capital city Arra by Ava Delphinus.

Post Ava's time, the constellations were extensively charted by the sisters. It is documented that they staged a constant star vigil on the roof of Salaina; the ancient Khean structure where the sisterhood lived and studied, learning all they could about the galaxy.

With their efforts The Sisterhood of Kalreene created the base clock and calendar for their planet, based up the works of Ava Delphinus, their own observations and that of the pioneer rew explorers who explored other planets using early solar sail ships during the first era of space travel.

The days of Rewna were first studied by Ava Delphinus, who identified there were 7 days in a typical Rewna week.

Ava used a numbering system to name them, however the sisters decided to name the days after the 7 animal guardian spirits of Rewna. Each of the animal guardians was rumoured to exist in a different biome and could only be seen by those were sought them to learn knowledge to use for a greater good.

1# Unoas – The Flight Worthy Guardian

A large golden bird of prey capable of circumnavigating Rewna in under an hour. It patrolled the skies of its planet, rarely ever landing except for nesting.

2# Tranai – The Horned Guardian

A large quadruped animal, Tranai had 5 horns and black heavily plated armour. Tranai inhabited the vast savannah of Ancient Rewna and is named as the first guardian to be encountered by early rew.

3# Meraca – The Oceanic Guardian
A pelagic dolphin like serpent creature with immense strength. It dived through the waters of the Blue Ocean on Ancient Rewna.

4# Biceries – The Clawed Guardian
Depicted as a large feathered quadruped with razor sharp claws which could supposedly shatter diamond. Biceries was originally the guardian of a heated volcanic biome that no longer exists.

5# Weanas – The River Guardian
A sea-fairy type creature who inhabits the rivers of Rewna. Almost sentient with its cognitive abilities, Weanas is also revered as the Spirit of Water.

6# Ultaria – The Polar Guardian
A bipedal leviathan covered in thick long white hair-like fur, Ultaria is also known by the name Momoso; the Khe word for frost giant. Friendly by behaviour, Ultaria wandered the southern polar region of Ancient Rewna.

7# Sonns – The Dark Guardian
The true appearance of Sonns has been lost to the ages. Rather The Dark Guardian is known by a sigil rather than appearance. It has been speculated that Sonns is the protector of the afterlife.

A Lasting Legacy

Unfortunately during The Unforgiving War from year -92 to the year -40, the efforts of Rewna's astronomers were mostly destroyed when the planet was targeted in order to kill nat-al and keoshi refugees taking shelter on Rewna.

Despite extensive bombardment during the war, some of Rewna's astronomy remained safe deep underground within Salaina's natural underground vault system. To this day the vault system continues to reveal its secrets, allowing archaeologists to re-learn Rewna's extensive history.

During the At War's End era following The Unforgiving War, the theories of The Sisterhood of Kalreene were used as the basis of the present day galactic clock and galactic year, with the galactic months and days used as a mean universal system for bringing a set constant to the galaxy, post horrors of the war.

The galactic clock uses the designation Galactic Standard Time (GST).

Due to different planets have differing year lengths, the galactic dating and clock system helps to simplify time zoning on a general cosmic scale. GST is used by a range of intergalactic-ranging organisations such as S.T.O.R.M and Galactic Mail as the mean time for operating against.

Space flight operators such as Tyerria Cosmic and Trans Skarmonia Spacelines, and independent spacecraft travelling the cosmos also use GST for space travel, especially between realms.

S.T.O.R.M's field operatives work on varied shift patterns dependant on mission lengths and frequency. GST is essential for ensuring the field operatives have their enforced break periods, known better as cold time, between mission periods. However it is a well documented fact that field operatives do try to cheat their cold time if they feel they've been given too much 'idle time' as it is sometimes called.

S.T.O.R.M COMMAND

S.T.O.R.M Command Call Sign Set

Alpha
Bravo
Charlie
Delta
Echo
Foxtrot
Gamma
Harrier
India
Juliet
Kilo
Lima
Mole
Nova
Oscar
Papa
Quasar
Romeo
Sierra
Tango
Udonna
Victor
Whiskey
Xenar
Yanka
Zulu

Branch Details:

Branch Colour: Eagle Yellow
Headquarters: Base Lempra, Tyerria
Field Operatives Known As: Mercies, Field Ops, All Rounders, Command

In Brief:

The first of the branches to be established as part of a major evolution for the organisation, S.T.O.R.M Command came into existence on 12th Kittapela 1949.

S.T.O.R.M Command is the core of the organisation, responsible for administration, Galactic Centre, the all rounder field operatives and overseeing the daily running of operations. Due to its responsibilities, it is also the largest of the 7 branches.

Typically it is the branch most sentients think of when the organisation is mentioned, possibly due to S.T.O.R.M Command featuring the original secondary colour and call sign set for its operatives.

All rounder field ops, or 'mercies', make up 50% of the featured field operatives partaking in the S.T.O.R.M Connect project, meaning they are the most seen online and in media.

Branch Responsibilities:

Out of all the branches, S.T.O.R.M Command has the most diverse range of operatives who join from all walks of life and from across all 12 realms. The branch also has the highest number of generational field ops and the second highest rate of students joining straight from educational studies behind S.T.O.R.M Medical.

S.T.O.R.M Command has 4 sub branches:

1. Administration
2. Galactic Centre
3. Field Command
4. Galaxy Access

The administration team, which ranges from station personnel to field operative branch chiefs, conduct the daily running of the organisation.

Galactic Centre is the core of S.T.O.R.M. Located deep beneath Base Lempra, the dome structure houses the primary response centre and geia designed supercomputer.

The geia oversee the running and maintenance of the supercomputer and its specialist software The Galactic Net; S.T.O.R.M's means of monitoring the galaxy. Smaller versions of

Galactic Centre are located at all primary and secondary S.T.O.R.M bases. Known as Orbital Centres during construction, they are named after their bases, with the exception of the 12 primaries, which are named after the realms they are located in.

Field Command focuses on the branch field operatives. In addition, it also deals with the responders who are often the first point of contact for sentients requiring S.T.O.R.M's assistance. Responders spend 6 months in training for their call duties whereas S.T.O.R.M Command field operatives will spend on average 2 – 4 years in the S.T.O.R.M Academy before joining the field.

Like all active S.T.O.R.M operatives, newly graduated mercies get to choose their call sign from a trio of suggestions, selected for them by S.T.O.R.M Academy's supercomputer 'The Eye of S.T.O.R.M'. If none of the call signs are to their liking, a new trio are selected, however this has never been the case.

Galaxy Access is linked to Administration, managing general public relations and projects including the S.T.O.R.M Museum, promoting of the S.T.O.R.M Connect project, and code blue extra-field missions run by ops of any branch as a means of engaging with the galaxy population at large.

S.T.O.R.M Command also plays an active role in assisting The Unity, helping to identify weak areas of travel and poor emergency response cover zones. As such S.T.O.R.M is helping shape the galaxy to become closer and more connected.

OPERATIVE PROFILE

*The following information is abridged from the S.T.O.R.M Galaxy Access Database and S.T.O.R.M Historical Archives.

Galactic Access Database
Field Operative Files

S.T.O.R.M DELTA ECHO
[4.D/E-Winters:Jack-COMMAND]

Call Sign: Delta Echo
Serial Number: TB41-D/E175.8.1
Branch: S.T.O.R.M Command
Given Name: Jack Winters
Date of Birth: 14th Aratha 2362
Place of Birth: Delta Echo Memorial Centre, Tyerria, Lempra Realm

Full Name:
   Jacqueline Qwenda Winters
Academy Start:
   29th Aratha 2373
Academy Graduation:
   8th Qwentas 2375

Present Status:
   Commander, Field Operative
Command:
   RPM Class Starship *Sweet Remedy*

Station Point:
   Eagle Station
Realm:
   Lempra
Estimated Rank Promotion:
   Jack Winters has stated on record that she will refuse any rank up for the foreseeable future on the basis she can do more as a commander.

Character Profile

Level-headed and strongly determined, Jack Winters is a formidable S.T.O.R.M field operative, considered by many to be amongst the greatest field operatives in S.T.O.R.M's history.

Jack has a reputation for being a mercie who just doesn't quit, showing a high level of commitment to S.T.O.R.M's cause and her duties. Jack has a proven high intellect that allows her to think outside the box and in a creative manner.

Humble and kind at heart, she understands what S.T.O.R.M means to children and often remains post mission if children are involved.

Yet despite this, Jack Winters isn't a simple open and cut sentient. Known for being quite jovial at the least expected moments, her sense of comedic timing often catches other operatives out, especially during missions. Jack is also known for having a flippant streak, something that usually manifests whilst she is recording a S.T.O.R.M Connect culinary vlog, or when the Jack Facts are mentioned.

Despite her exaggerated reputation she is amongst the shiest and quietest of Eagle Station's field operatives. More often than not she can be found on her starship between missions, either playing digigames, tinkering with her starship or recording S.T.O.R.M Connect vlogs. She also clocks a number of hours in the Go Sportivate gym each week, practising her skills in the shooting range and challenging other ops to assault course runs.

Jack is known to regularly play multiplayer games, notably critically acclaimed *S.T.O.R.M Galactic Heroes*; a galactic wide multiplayer game based on S.T.O.R.M file operative missions, for which she is a missions consultant for. She has a preference for motorsport games, regularly recording her play-time for S.T.O.R.M Connect.

A loyal friend, dedicated to a fault and an enthusiast of engineering classic and new, Jack also has a keen interest in zoology and frequently volunteers for research missions.

She holds the given title of 'the galaxy's favourite hero', first used by the general public in early 2382. Jack is galactically well-liked and admired. Her unofficial fan club, The Delta Echo Fan Club, has 129.9 trillion members spanning the range of the cosmos.

In the negative, Jack has a short fuse when dealing with violence. This manifests in Jack's enforcement of The Guardian Angel Accords where is she known to take harsher action against anybody who breaches them. Her more aggressive stance often results in physical action. Her temper will also flare if her starship or the RPM Class is criticised unfairly.

Jack is notorious for not saying goodbye and for making hot beverages only to forget about them, letting them go stone cold. Her culinary skills are also seen in a negative light thanks to her exploits in vlogs for the S.T.O.R.M Connect project. Whilst she admits she can cook, she refuses to be any good at it.

Field Operative History

Born on Tyerria to Erika and Bill Winters, Jack Winters and her parents moved to the ill-fated space station *April Falls* when she was 2 years old.

Her parents were both doctors; her mother a specialist in neurology and her father a specialist in family medicine and trauma.

On 20th Manas 2368, *April Falls* suffered a catastrophic environmental systems failure. Erika Winters was killed however Bill and Jack managed to survive, Jack was found and rescued by S.T.O.R.M Foxtrot Alpha (Carson Feldman) after she was separated from her father during the chaos.

Leading on from the tragedy and death of his wife, Bill Winters joined S.T.O.R.M. Not wanting to be separated from her father, Jack became a S.T.O.R.M brat, staying by his side for the first 4 months. As Bill progressed with his training, Jack joined her paternal grandparents, Julia and Shane Winters, on the planet Hegaldia in the Far Reach System.

On Hegaldia, Jack's interest in zoology took root. She assisted her grandparents with their conservation efforts protecting the critically endangered thunderbirds; a large, indigenous bird of prey almost wiped out by disease and poaching. Jack became a skilled tracker of the birds, befriending several thunderbirds including a breeding pair who allowed her into their nest. Most notably, Jack befriended a young male thunderbird named Sisko whom she nursed back to health.

During this period Jack learnt to fly, quickly mastering her grandparents gliders, microlights and stratabikes. She applied herself in mechanics and repaired their old T4-Series helicopter with her older cousin, Tiff Winters.

Upon her father's graduation at the start of 2370, Bill moved to Hawk Station in the Remida Realm, immediately joining a pack of operatives led by veteran S.T.O.R.M Mole Udonna (Shauna Dawkin) on the Rapid Class starship *Mighty Maiden*. Jack joined her father, bar her holiday visits to her grandparents, wherein Shauna took her under her wing, becoming something of a mother figure to her.

Even before she joined the S.T.O.R.M Academy, Jack had made quite the name for herself. Bill enrolled his daughter in S.T.O.R.M's Junior Rescue Corps, upon realising she would follow him into S.T.O.R.M. She took to the JRC with great vigour, excelling in every challenge given to her and surprising her instructors. All of them agreed that Jack was destined to join S.T.O.R.M Command and would become a formidable mercie in the future.

Shauna gave Jack additional practice at the helm of her command and taught her about starship engineering; an area Jack took a keen interest in and soon knew the Rapid Class like the back of her hand. She routinely surprised everybody with her advanced intellect. Jack continued to hone her piloting finesse on *Mighty Maiden* and with gliders and stratabikes on Hegaldia.

During a return flight home on 3rd Yyenn 2370, Shauna's pack were knocked out by a sonic wave. Jack being a child was unaffected by it. She managed to navigate the ship through a solar storm and send out a distress call. Jack also guided the starship to a rendezvous point with another S.T.O.R.M starship impressing everyone with her natural flaw for handling herself in tough situations. She received S.T.O.R.M's civilian Golden Star Award for bravery.

By the time she was ready to leave for the S.T.O.R.M Academy, Jack had clocked 692 hours piloting *Mighty Maiden,* setting a new flight record for a S.T.O.R.M Junior Rescue Corps scout; a record that still stands to this date.

On 29th Aratha 2373, Jack joined the S.T.O.R.M Academy, having graduated from the S.T.O.R.M Junior Rescue Corps with flying colours. During the 2 months of theory work, the instructors nicknamed Jack 'the fidgeter' as she struggled to keep still.

It was during this time that Jack formed a close friendship with fellow trainee Wynona Sorbonne.

Having met her on their induction day, the duo were coincidentally assigned living quarters together. Wynona, a 15 year old former sex slave from the L'Xarian System, was surprised by Jack's laid back and open-minded attitude to others, even after Wynona told Jack her past. This knowledge and trust made Jack even more protective of her declared 'best friend'.

In the academy Jack made a name for herself for a multitude of reasons; some good and some bad.

She established herself as a force to be reckoned with, showcasing a high intellect and creative thought process. Her piloting became the envy of the academy, with her mastery of piloting the academy starships earning her attention from outside the academy.

Collectively Wynona and Jack became a formidable duo of demmies as their training progressed – something not lost on their instructors.

After 8 months in the academy, the pair of them were tipped by their main instructor to become mercies, owing to their ingenuity and quick adaptability. Wynona's medical proficiency and Jack's engineering prowess made them perfect pack-mates.

Such was Jack's impact in particular on S.T.O.R.M, she prompted changes to several procedures after she found more efficient ways of preforming them. She also picked up on a small glitch with the new Tornado Class weapons guidance system, much to the annoyance of the class creator.

Yet her success also earned her a healthy bout of jealousy from other demmies. Other demmies were quick to see Jack as a rival, jealous of her perceived perfectness and routinely looking for ways to trip her up, celebrating whenever she messed up.

To her credit Jack didn't rise to the bait. However when fellow trainees started insulting Wynona to get a rise out of Jack, she was unable to ignore them, Jack started fighting back, even provoking her main antagonists on purpose, much to the chargain of her instructors and Wynona who tried to rein her in.

This resulted in numerous fist fights and reprimands from instructors, plus a stern talking to from her father and Shauna. Things came to a head as the insults towards Wynona continued.

Jack refused to take a back seat approach and broke academy rules to lay an ambush for the main antagonists, luring them to one of the dry docks, wherein Jack, outnumbered 9-1, took out all of the gang using clever tricks and Vikirian Army brawling tactics. The fight was broken up by the S.T.O.R.M Academy and S.T.O.R.M Military chiefs.

Despite having broken the academy rules by striking other trainees with intent to cause harm and deliberately tampering with academy security systems, it was concluded that Jack was only trying to protect her best friend and that her often unorthodox methods and creative thinking were a key part of her work ethnic. Jack was let off the hook with a reprimand, but she served 2 months of clean up duty at the S.T.O.R.M Guard facilities; a duty that put her off ever teaming up with a guardie.

Jack entered active service just over 2 years later on 8th Qwentas 2375, graduating at the same time as Wynona. Both of them joined S.T.O.R.M Command with Jack taking the call sign Delta Echo out of the choices Delta Echo, Nova Delta and India Delta. The decision was an easy choice for Jack who, knowing the illustrious history for the first choice, and wanting a shot at making it her own.

Jack and Wynona were assigned to Pelican Station in the Skarmonia Realm where in they immediately branched off with the highly regarded Bravo Zulu (Miko Ashington), after Wynona got them lost in Pelican Station's docking ring. Miko was between starships, borrowing older starships between them being assigned permanent operators. At the time of meeting Jack and Wynona, he was looking after the Tornado Class *Rapid Charge*.

Right from the off, Jack began to develop a reputation for doing the impossible. Her first engineering miracle came when she improvised lightspeed engine components for use in emergency open heart surgery.

Hopping from starship to starship, the trio partnered together for a number of missions, developing a reputation for being unorthodox yet versatile and professional field operatives.

On 19th Quoistas 2375, the trio were sent on an important scientific mission to Corbett's Point within the Tornado Nebula, located on the far edge of the Skarmonia Realm.

Due to the high delta radiation levels of the Tornado Nebula, it was impossible for any regular starship to pass through. The Rapid Class *Sapphire Blue* had to be heavily modified to make the trip, with Jack making a large number of the modifications herself, impressing the engineering teams on Lantos.

The trio spent a month gathering information on the region. During their time they acquired the first up-close readings of the Delphinus Diamond, a small comet that passes close to the edge of the galaxy every 400 years, amongst other research. Their mission was a resounding success, prompting their names to be inducted onto The Science Order of Honours List.

In mid 2376 'the terrific trio', as they'd been dubbed by other field operatives, transferred to Eagle Station in the Lempra Realm, giving the Discovery Class *Final Roar* a shakedown en route.

Continuing their starship hopping ways, they hooked up with Sierra Tango (Kel Williams) and Zulu Golf (Midnight Goodwill) after the veteran duo sent out a distress call regarding a code red mission on the 10th Serath. The group ended up becoming pack-mates aboard Midnight's Rapid Class starship *Soaring Wing*. The unlikely pack would remain together for the next 5 years.

On 20th Repaba 2376, Jack was introduced to future S.T.O.R.M Operations Director S.T.O.R.M Tango Delta (Sara Narusha) after

Soaring Wing is sent to assist Sara's pack on the planet Rhetqui during a settlement rebuild.

Recognising each other from their colourful back-and-forth exchanges on the S.T.O.R.M Forums, Sara was quick to insult Jack. In turn Jack responded with an easy retort, calling her the Director's pet. This prompted Kel to spit his orange sports drink out laughing. However beneath the surface friction was a deep level of respect and admiration for each other.

In 2377 Jack achieved the rank of lieutenant, aged 15. In doing so she broke the 90 year record for youngest human field operative to achieve the rank, beating the previous record by 14 months and 12 days.

Jack began recording vlogs in 2379 for the S.T.O.R.M Connect project. From there she became a well known face to the general public at large. Her vlogs initially centred on her life as a mercie, spreading out into more comedic topics. Jack soon developed a reputation for her outrageous cooking antics, multiplayer digigames antics and badly drawn comedic sketches.

In early 2381, Sara Narusha was appointed Eagle Station & Lempra Realm Chief. Much to Jack's chargain, she began changing operational procedures, resulting in a number of clashes between the pair. Their routine arguments quickly became popular amongst fellow Eagle Station field ops, with Jack deliberately going out of her way to provoke Sara when she felt changes were unnecessary.

On 21st Serath 2381, Midnight officially retired from active field duty. *Soaring Wing* was to be decommissioned, however Midnight insisted on retaining the starship for her new instructor role at the S.T.O.R.M Academy.

This left Jack, Kel, Wynona and Miko without a starship. The following day Kel was offered the 2 year old Discovery Class starship *Graceful Angel*. The terrific trio joined him for the short period of 6 days before Jack received a priority call from the Operations Director at Base Lempra. She was told to report to Lantos.

On 30th Serath 2381, Jack was presented with her own starship; the brand new RPM Class *Sweet Remedy*. The decision was deemed necessary by the Operations Director of the time, stating that Jack's brilliance necessitated her operating her own starship, rather than being a junior member of a pack.

The sixth RPM Class off the line, *Sweet Remedy* was the first of her class to arrive at Eagle Station. She prompted a great deal of interest, even more so when it was revealed the new starship was a COSS (Custom Order Specification Starship), as per ordered by the Operations Director.

Jack continued to team up with Miko and Wynona, running missions alongside Kel in *Graceful Angel* on a regular basis. She also began running missions with the Val'Kii SAS, having built up a strong relationship with senior officer Major General Jojoan Mass, assisting them with various calls, much to Kel and Bill's concern.

On 4th Aratha 2381, aged 20, Jack's popularity sky-rocketed when she took centre stage in a celebrity scandal. On a rare non-command enforced day off, she ended up arresting a well known sportsman.

3x galactic champion racing pilot Rakellan Marius was giving a press conference outside The Tyerria Halls of Motor Racing, surrounded by many adorning fans, including a number of young children. Jack happened to walk past whilst on her way to get breakfast. Children recognised her and she found herself swamped by excited fans.

Angry someone had dared to steal his thunder, Rakellan decided to approach Jack and threatened to attack her. Knowing his history of violence and that because of his status he'd gotten away with it, Jack defended herself by breaking his nose and arresting him. This time he was held accountable for his actions and made to serve 560 hours of community service.

The resulting media attention drew heavy focus to Jack, transforming her from just another field operative into a galactically recognised hero. Her S.T.O.R.M Connect vlogs hit record levels and her starship was added to the Spacecraft Watcher's Guide.

Jack found her new found fame initially off-putting, but she came to realise it had its advantages in terms of boosting morale. As such Jack increased the flamboyancy of her cooking vlogs and other material, much to be bemusement of other operatives. A petition was jokingly started complaining of Jack's treatment of pastries.

This was actually taken seriously and brought before the Operations Director who dismissed it immediately, instead authorising a supply of low yield explosives for Jack to use for future videos.

The following week Jack almost blew a hole in her starship's top deck using explosive putty mixed pancakes.

The Fine Lines Months

On 7th Manas 2382, Wynona's field career came to an abrupt ending. Jack and Wynona were helping track down a pregnant Destran Tiger in a wildlife sanctuary on Tyerria when the creature attacked them, ripping out Wynona's guts. Jack managed to fend off the endangered creature and save Wynona's life but the encounter signalled the end to her field career. Instead Wynona opted to assist Sara Narusha as her second in command, effectively taking over the running of Eagle Station.

The sanctuary incident was the first of many high casualty missions where S.T.O.R.M field operatives were either killed or suffered close fatalities over a period of several months.

Spanning from Manas 2382 to Jawe 2383, S.T.O.R.M would later in life refer to as this period as 'The Fine Line Months'. In total, 245 operatives were killed during this period; the second highest ever mortality period since the inception of S.T.O.R.M and in its entire history bar The Tyerria Repulsion.

Jack herself faced a number of difficult missions which saw her face serious injuries and the deaths of other field operatives, and face notable difficult missions. It also saw Jack's call sign prominently highlighted by the press on several missions which were made public knowledge for one reason or another.

Jack was noted to have been highly active during this period, often covering for other field operatives and assisting the Val'Kii SAS and RFRC with call outs. She also played a major role in coordinating operations during Storm Palia.

The Diabolos Massacre on Crissa Prime

On 15th Manas 2382, after escaping from the high security detention facility Evelon Guard Sanctuary, mass murderer Michael Crossroad sent a distress call from a famine stricken village on the planet Syti, deliberately to lure S.T.O.R.M to the scene. His plan worked; before anyone knew what had happened, he'd killed 3 S.T.O.R.M operatives and massacred 19 villagers.

Knowing what would ensue, Crossroad barricaded himself in an abandoned mill, taking 29 hostages, including 2 rookie gennies. Jack was part of a team that entered the structure, but was deceived by a booby trap and nearly killed.

Taken hostage, Crossroad goaded about killing Jack due to her 'celebrity' status. She was next to be killed by Crossroad when a joint

S.T.O.R.M – Val'Kii SAS team ambushed the structure, killing Crossroad and saving most of the survivors. The duo of rookie operatives were killed in crossfire.

Crash Landing on Remorgah

On 29th Manas, *Sweet Remedy* suffered catastrophic engine failure after a faulty replacement part exploded. Jack was forced to crash land on Remorgah in the Cheltas System. Luckily she was able to angle her ship towards Inaot Landing Port and crash landed on runway 3. The resulting crash flooded *Sweet Remedy* with toxic gases and it was only due to the quick thinking of runway emergency crews and Jack reaching her EVC helmet that she survived.

At the time of the crash she had been responding to a code red call when she developed engine trouble. She would spend 2 months piloting the RPM Class *Mystic Thunderbird* whilst *Sweet Remedy* was overhauled and the faulty unit investigated.

Jack took the younger starship on as her operator S.T.O.R.M Tango Quasar (Jenni Tarana) had been killed 2 weeks prior. Jack and Jenni had become close friends over the years and Jack took her death badly.

Storm Palia

On 12th Kittapela 2382, a sun storm erupted from the sun in the Grey Sun System. The unanticipated event saw an initially slow response putting trillions of lives in jeopardy.

Jack was on call in the neighbouring Rover System when she heard about the cosmic event. Immediately she activated Stormguard Protocol and oversaw rescue efforts across the Remida Realm, coordinating the RFRC and Val'Kii SAS to reach those who needed help. She was highly commended for her actions and efforts and was later knighted by the Talago royal family.

Sera Taisha

On 22nd Yyenn 2383, Jack and Miko ran into difficulty on a code red rescue mission on Sera Taisha. They'd responded to a mayday from a downed transport ship that had suffered engine failure and been forced to crash land on the planet.

Hundreds of lives were in danger and so Jack put out a code white distress call. In total 42 field operatives responded, along with 53 officers of the Val'Kii SAS. The co-op team managed to save 70% of all passengers and crew. The mission however resulted in Miko's death.

Jack blamed herself for the incident, throwing herself back into her duties. After reading the reports, and despite not being there due to his S.T.O.R.M Academy instructor role, Kel had S.T.O.R.M Medical rule Jack unfit for duty. She was reinstated a week later after veteran mercie, Tango Yanka (Aryan Hardi), took her on a needed mountain climbing break.

Kel's actions however had a lasting impact, costing him Jack's trust and respect. Upon realising he was responsible for her removal, Jack confronted Kel over his actions, resulting in a physical altercation between the once-friends. The duo wouldn't speak to each for other over a year.

The Firestorm Oil Slick on Aquiata

On 29th Das 2383, Jack responded to an environmental disaster on Aquiata. A cargo hauler had fallen from orbit and caused a planetary oil slick. Numerous rescuers from S.T.O.R.M, the Val'Kii SAS and The Remida Fire and Rescue Corps partook in the clean up.

The event drew galactic attention as the organisations pulled together their resources. For a duration they looked to be succeeding.

However further disaster struck when a civilian amphibious craft became trapped in the oil, causing its engines to overheat and explode.

The resulting explosion spread like wildfire turning the planet into a ferocious fireball, vaporising hundreds of relief workers in the flames. Jack herself was lucky to survive when the heatwave struck *Sweet Remedy*, her life support systems and shielding protecting her and her operator.

Aquiata was rendered virtually lifeless in the firestorm. Incredibly not a single S.T.O.R.M operative was killed during the disaster, owing to their advanced EVC suits and helmets which withstood the heat. The disaster is considered to be the unofficial ending of The Fine Line Months.

Post The Fine Line Months

On 3rd Karnao 2384, Jack was promoted to lieutenant commander and was awarded The White Star Cross for bravery. Initially she declined it but upon the insistence of other ops, she accepted, if anything to not incur their wrath.

With Wynona now settled into her role as Lempra Realm and Eagle Station chief, a sense of normality resumed to Jack's life.

Early in 2385, Jack teamed up with S.T.O.R.M Harrier Victor (Benjamin Cutter) with whom she had a brief romantic relationship. Benjamin called it off when it became clear to him that Jack was completely dedicated towards S.T.O.R.M and would remain with the organisation for life.

Benjamin called Jack out on the S.T.O.R.M Forums, stating boldly that she would only leave when she was killed on the job. He had been hoping to do the job for a few years then call it quits. With that, he called the relationship off. Other field operatives were quick to round on him and defend Jack, but the damage had been done.

Jack became emotionally aloof, dismissive of other ops and her starship's maintenance. This resulted in the near-destruction of *Sweet Remedy* during a standard code blue research mission. The incident served as a wake up call to Jack, who vowed never to disregard *Sweet Remedy* again.

Over the remainder of the year Jack fell into a routine of operating solo, enjoying the peace and quiet. Multiple operatives, including Wynona, Sara and her father, attempted to get her to form a pack of her own, but Jack kept resisting.

This changed at the start of 2386 when Jack invited her younger cousin S.T.O.R.M Mole Alpha (Syd Winters) to join her, post Syd's graduation ceremony from the S.T.O.R.M Academy. Syd accepted Jack's offer and the cousins teamed up for 2 years until Syd felt ready to move onto new challenges, moving to the Skarmonia Realm.

In the tail end of 2386, Kel returned to Eagle Station, resuming his regular duties. Wynona made a note to responders not to pair Jack and Kel up on missions. The following year Jack began co-oping on missions with Sara when she returned to Eagle Station. The duo called a 'truce' as it were, enjoying each other's company on calls.

During the summer of 2387, Jack extended an apple branch to Kel, both of them wishing to put the past behind them. Gradually Jack had started trusting him again, the clincher being when Kel saved her from *Sweet Remedy* after a toxic gas cannister ruptured, risking his own life to save Jack.

On 23rd Qwentas 2387, Jack was promoted to the rank of Commander and offered a second ship, the much larger Discovery Class *Flying Beauty*. She declined in favour of running *Sweet Remedy,* stating that she didn't need the additional space and that she couldn't imagine running a different starship.

Jack did however accept a mission instructor role within the academy. Over the following 10 months she created over 40 new simulations and mock missions. She also played an active role in training up 16 trainees, this in addition to fulfilling her regular duties in the Lempra Realm.

Whilst on call in late 2388, Jack was moved to tears when she found out Syd had joined the pack that operated *Mystic Thunderbird*. Syd herself had become a prolific pilot of the RPM Class, acknowledging Jack as her tutor.

In the latter part of 2389 Jack resumed her full regular duties, accepting a couple of rookie mercies she'd trained up. They remained with Jack until the end of the year before moving to stations in the Artelaine and Evelon Realms.

In 2390, Jack went back to flying solo, occasionally accepting other operatives as guests and teaming up on missions with Kel with his ever changing pack. *Sweet Remedy* often served alongside Kel's starship, the Discovery Class *Graceful Angel*. Jack also undertook a number of research missions, alongside her Val'Kii SAS work.

Jack's solo habit once again changed in 2393 when she accepted relative newcomer S.T.O.R.M India Juliet (Harmony Alonso) as a 'temporary' pack-mate. However, after 14 missions together, it was obvious that their partnership would last considerably longer, much to Jack's apparent annoyance.

6 weeks into their formalised pack life, Jack and Harmony accepted millie S.T.O.R.M Yeovil Nervis (Rikos Lander) as a semi-regular pack-mate, the 44 year old millie fitting right in with the younger ops.

As of the start of 2395, Jack continues in her field operative role in command of *Sweet Remedy*. Frequently Jack and Harmony run missions alongside Kel Williams and his new charge Bravo Victor (Turiso Duski-Hectori).

On 6th Quoistas 2395 during an interview at The Galactic Rescue Show on Tyerria, Jack publicly shot down rumours she and Rikos were dating, citing the Eagle Station veterans as being 'absolute buggars for winding her up'.

Additional Notes

Jack is the fourth S.T.O.R.M field operative to hold the call sign Delta Echo. Prior to Jack taking it for herself, 16 other field operatives were offered and declined the call sign.

Throughout her career Jack has had strong ties to the Val'Kii SAS, having many friendships within the organisation. Due to her close ties, she frequently runs co-op missions. She is listed as an honorary officer of the Val'Kii SAS.

On 1st Manas 2386, Jack was granted euthanasia status by The Galactic Medical Council, meaning she is authorised to put down sentients who are beyond saving.

Jack is fluent in a number of languages including Alingu, Kleshi and Zaraka. She can seamlessly alternate between Alingu and Kleshi (language of the Val'Kii).

Like all field operatives, Jack is fluent in Universal Sign Language (USL). Jack considers Kleshi to be her second language and is notorious on Eagle Station for teaching rookie field operatives Kleshi profanity. Jack is also fluent in starship code; owing to her background in spacecraft engineering.

Jack is known for being an avid fan of The Galactic Championship. She is an enthusiastic supporter of underdogs RPM Auto and has attended numerous races as a VIP guest. For the past 4 years she has had the honour of handing over the winner's trophy.

On several occasions Jack has been called upon to defend the RPM Class in light of apparent design flaws.

The most notable defence came about in 2392 when a hidden bug in the safety mode prompted the apparent reactivation of the mode during active flight. Jack identified an extra wire in the command computer of the affected starship, the 3 years old *Soaring Heights*, recognising the handiwork of an unknown source. It was later proven the child of a field operative was attempting to 'help' by using the starship as a science homework project.

Jack holds a quintet of degrees. Her first degree for zoology and conversation she picked up from The Tyerria Biological Sciences University in 2379. She acquired her engineering degrees from The Teyressia Science Academy. Her first was in 2384 for spacecraft design and technology, and her second degree in advanced engineering in 2387. Her fourth and firth degrees were honorary from the The Tyerria Advanced Engineering School and Royal Skarmonia University. They are in spacecraft design and rescue studies respectively.

Jack's S.T.O.R.M Connect channel is called Delta Echo 4. At present it has 254 trillion subscribers galactically, making it the third most subscribed social media channel in the Delphinus Galaxy and the most popular S.T.O.R.M channel of all.

L - #0233 - 021220 - C0 - 175/108/10 - PB - DID2970482